Darkenbane:

The Fountain

Darkenbane:

The Fountain

Kimberly Adkins

Black Lyon Publishing, LLC

DARKENBANE: THE FOUNTAIN

Our books may be ordered through your local bookstore or by visiting the publisher:

www.BlackLyonPublishing.com

Black Lyon Publishing, LLC
PO Box 567
Baker City, OR 97814

ISBN-10: 1-934912-05-0
ISBN-13: 978-1-934912-05-8
Library of Congress Control Number: 2008929040

Written, published and printed in the United States of America.

Black Lyon Paranormal Romance

For my best friend, Julie,
truly a beautiful flower in the garden of life.

Introduction

She could barely see over the edge of her mother's dressing table, kneeling on the padded chair in front of the vanity as she was. The pots and vials of cosmetics came together in a sparkling presentation of mysterious temptations as the young girl reached very carefully among the jars. Though she had slipped out of the care of her servant girl when she knew her noble parents were involved in an important gathering at the great hall, she still felt nervous about being apprehended with her mother's fine things.

The court alchemist's station couldn't have presented her with more trouble as she tried in vain to identify pieces of the collection before her, so her tiny fingers grasped the nearest familiar item. With great care, the girl lifted the heavy, ivory brush and slowly touched the stiff bristles to her dark, unruly hair. She smiled immediately at her reflection, her green eyes nearly cresting the bottom of the looking glass. Though her family had many serving women to brush her hair each night, her mother often took the time to complete the task herself with gentle, caring hands and the routine always calmed her thoughts.

With no such experience to guide the bristles, her attempt at taming the wild curls on her head might have made them worse; still, she felt satisfied that she had completed an important ritual and climbed gingerly down from the cushioned bench.

The guest chambers where her family had been stationed were fine, but the tension in the air was palpable, even to her sheltered senses. They had arrived a few precious days earlier, but those days gave the clever girl time enough to learn the ins and outs of their living quarters as the adults around her went about their business with a feeling of strained urgency.

She smoothed her dress carefully, as she had seen her mother do before her parents were called away to meet with the other important families of the realm.

With the curiosity of the young, and possible answers to the secrets of whispering servants waiting, she left the chamber quietly to explore the castle of the High King while everyone seemed to be involved with the big discussion. In her innocent quest for answers she didn't notice the deathly stillness that often comes before the storm, or focus enough to mark the path she had taken along the dry and deserted stone corridors of the eerily silent keep.

The alcove she stumbled into was nearly hidden; a great secret, she imagined with delight, but nothing eclipsed the discovery that lay on the other side of the antechamber.

A small and intimate courtyard broke free of the surrounding stone that made up the fortification of the castle. A cool breeze stirred her hair from her shoulders and she looked up to see the sky filled with heavy, grey clouds. In the center of the small area was a beautiful stone fountain, with three tiers of elaborately carved designs and symbols she didn't recognize. A wild vine grew throughout the courtyard, easily over taking the stone benches and sculpted statues that decorated this peaceful place. Somehow, she knew it had been a long time since anyone had been to this secluded, secret garden.

The water in the fountain flowed freely and bubbled in an almost entrancing way as it splashed into the bottom level. She stepped lightly over the vines that had taken hold on the flagstones underneath her slippers, and noticed the dizzying scent of the small white and purple flowers they supported.

She was not tall enough to sit on the rim of the lowest tier, so she leaned over the side in an attempt to see her reflection. The waves distorted her image there and almost threw her off balance. She gasped for a moment in wonder as her face seemed to change before her very eyes, becoming that of a beautiful young woman, not unlike an image of her mother. The instant she reached forth her fingertips to touch this vision in the waves, a polite cough was issued from behind. She abruptly stood, her cheeks flaming red as if she were caught doing something she should not.

"What is a lady doing out on the grounds unescorted?" The voice clearly belonged to that of a young man, and she stood as commandingly tall as possible when she turned.

Whatever words she had been preparing in her defense slipped away and she felt a strange tingle somewhere deep inside. The newcomer stood at attention in what was surely military dress, but his smile was easy and his blue eyes sparkled with warm delight. Though he would have been just a few short years older than she was, he seemed very handsome and dashing in her limited experience.

"Forgive me." He looked a little flustered, and his blush betrayed his young age. As he extended one hand towards her, the sun escaped the thick blanket of clouds overhead and fell onto his golden hair when he inclined his head. "If I may introduce myself, I am Edward."

Her hand seemed to move forward of its own volition and set itself in his upturned palm. He bowed slightly over her offering, but made no other contact.

"I was just ... " She hesitated slightly, looking around for some kind of excuse. "I was just looking at your fountain! Because it is much nicer than my fountain ... The one at my castle ... "

He nodded at her in the way people do to humor a child, and released her fingers to motion her back in the direction of the water-filled centerpiece. He sat easily on the edge she had so longed for a short time ago, but she joined him readily, standing near.

"This is a very special fountain." He looked wistfully into the ripples below. "One that I am told will hold my destiny."

"What is your destiny?" she asked, wide-eyed at his statement.

"A destiny must be discovered, my beautiful young girl." He chuckled in a worldly manner that must have been his own answer to that very question, many times over.

"Might I ask your name?" he asked suddenly, looking directly at her. The attention, coupled with that question, caused her cheeks to redden again, more deeply this time.

"You nearly blush the color of this jasmine," he said gently, and she looked down to see the dark pink flowers at her feet.

"Yes, Jasmine," her voice echoed his last word, unable to focus her thoughts as she bent down to touch the fragrant bloom with distraction.

Thunder crashed heavily above them. The delicate blossom of the flower she had been stroking broke off in her hand at the upstart, and she felt a terrible guilt that she had so quickly plucked it. The air grew dark and filled with a sharp, acrid odor. Her new friend looked up from the fountain in confusion, just as the screams broke out.

"Come with me, quickly!" He only hesitated for a moment, as awareness suddenly struck. Without waiting for her consent, he grabbed her hand tightly and pulled her away from the courtyard and into the alcove. Once inside the small chamber, he stepped in front of her, his right arm extended behind him to press her safely against the wall. Cautiously, the brave young man peered from the door way, though she could feel him tremble slightly because his touch never left her.

Shock waves rippled through the thick stone once more, and the air became even more unbearable to breathe. Dust crumbled down from the ceiling overhead in drizzles and Edward grabbed her hand once more. Every fiber in her being screamed out for her to run, but he pressed on slowly, carefully, and she was forced to follow his lead. They neared the guest quarters and he turned quickly, grabbing her by the shoulders.

"Which one of these is yours?" he asked urgently, but in her terror she couldn't recall. She froze at the sound of pounding footsteps advancing on them, their growing echo along the corridor giving them away. Edward drew his training sword and stepped in front of her, nearly impaling her serving girl as she rounded the corner in haste.

"Your Highness," the servant gasped when she laid eyes on the young man, forgetting her task at hand for the moment. "Your father needs you at his side immediately!"

Edward's face show signs of emotional conflict and he looked earnestly at the young girl he had been protecting.

"I must first complete my duty here," he said simply, offering no apology as he took her small hand again.

"Her mother is just inside," the unfortunate woman said cautiously, not sure how to argue with the son of a King. "You must let her go if she is to get away."

He carefully looked her in the eyes and time seemed to slow as he regarded her features. He nodded almost imperceptibly at the woman, convinced he saw the truth in her words.

"I will take you as far as your quarters, then," he conceded and immediately put the child between himself and the maid. When they arrived at her rooms, he knelt before her on one knee as the woman opened the door.

"Do not fear," he said firmly. "I will return to you when I can."

She nodded and mustered up a trembling smile at his words. With a soft kiss on her forehead, he stood and watched them enter the chamber as he resisted the urge to run to his father's aid. Years of training allowed him to cautiously move away from his charge and disappear down the hall with calculated care.

"Quickly, now," her mother immediately instructed the nursemaid who brought her daughter inside. "Why is she still in her noble dressing gown? You know the Prophecy states that a girl child of noble birth will be the downfall of the Brotherhood! If they find her like that ... "

"My Lady Miriam, I fear for any young girl they find today," the frightened servant answered. Before the child knew what was happening, she was stripped of most of her fine garments and dressed in the rags of a beggar. Her mother adjusted a large, circular ring of silver which hung on the wall at the far end of the room. The confused girl thought it was perhaps another mirror, but as it was touched here and there, it shimmered like a live pool of water. She struggled on the lap of the woman who held her still in front of the vanity, eager to be near her mother and fearful for the safety of her absent father.

"It is almost ready," the noble woman whispered to her trusted servant. "The books were taken to safety and we must swiftly follow their passage."

A deep boom echoed through the stone of the castle once more, and the girl turned to look in the mirror of the dressing table she had so longed to view before. There, for a brief second before the ceiling collapsed, she saw herself as she was just hours ago, pulling a heavy brush through her massive curls. The wave passed and the room was torn apart.

Fire broke out between the curtains and carpeting in the room. The smoke was oily and black, and she instinctively knew not to breathe it in. She stood in the center of the room covered in dust, ash and dressed in rags.

"Take her!" her mother cried from beneath a part of the broken stone wall. Her caretaker seemed frozen in place. Her eyes were drawn inexorably to the unstable, rippling surface of the ring on the wall.

"I will do what I can for her! Take her through now," the noble woman commanded. The air heated to an unbearable level and it was difficult to breathe. With an urgent motion, she was lifted easily by the frightened servant and taken to the ring. She turned to see her mother near the fire, crying but with a smile on her face so that she wouldn't be afraid.

"I will do what I can for you," she promised, and the child clasped tighter the silky petals from the fountain as everything grew dark around her.

Chapter One

Jasmine sat up in bed, her breath tearing through her lungs in great gasps. It was the dream again, always the same dream. A deep sheen of perspiration glistened on her skin in the eerie green glow of the hotel alarm clock. For so many years she tried to discover the reason for the nighttime disruptions, to see if there was a pattern to the madness locked somewhere inside. She released her long, slender legs from the entangling sheets at the foot of the bed and stood on the unfamiliar carpet. The clock said 2:04 AM, and she pulled the curtains aside to see what she could see of the city at this hour.

Her hotel was situated on Canal Street, just across from the French Quarter in New Orleans. She was several stories high, and though she was behind tinted windows in the dark, she felt as if a thousand eyes from the city were watching her. The glass reached from the floor to nearly the ceiling, and she touched her fingers against the cool surface to lean forward.

The French Quarter was set up for her bird's eye view in all its glory. Tight little blocks of antiquated buildings lined up in the darkness, quietly holding their own against the neon lights of Bourbon Street and the tourists who lurked there looking for a thrill.

A small shiver, perhaps of anticipation, escalated up her spine. She had read about New Orleans before coming, but nothing could have prepared her for the feelings that stirred deep inside as she came near it. If she had ever seen this city before, she didn't remember it. In fact, she remembered nothing about her early childhood before the kindly couple in California adopted her and took her in as a part of their family. They never pretended she was their biological child, but they often told her that they couldn't have been blessed with a better daughter. All they knew about her was her name. The only question she had ever been able to answer was that, and when asked, it was always "Jasmine."

The mystery of who she was and where she came from was not allowed to interfere with her life and her family while growing up, but the shadow of the dream always hung over her head, and because of it, she never felt quite like she belonged. When she turned eighteen years-old, her parents did their best to try to find something about her past to comfort her, anything at all. They were never able to discover any information, and when she turned twenty-one, she tried herself, just to make sure. She was told same things they told her adopted parents years before. That she was off the grid, with no leads and no identification. She didn't exist before she was found wandering in the parking lot of the Louisiana hospital the night of her discovery.

"Of course I don't even remember that." She frowned bitterly, and realized she had rested her forehead and the main part of her body against the cold, air conditioned window. When she pulled away, a strange, steamy outline formed on the glass for a brief second and seemed to reach its hands high above in a plea for answers.

The ghost of me, she thought silently as the fragile image faded away against the night sky of the city.

Jasmine breathed a sigh of resignation, well aware that no matter what she did, sleep wouldn't be an option for the rest of the night. The dream would stay in her head until the small hours of the dawn, as if it couldn't allow her to forget one single thing until the sunlight made the world seem real again.

But this whole trip was surreal, and everything that had happened to her in the past two weeks was difficult to understand, let alone accept.

She reached inside the secure zipper pocket of her suitcase and pulled out the heavy, long envelope that had been opened and closed so many times that the flap was in serious danger of facing an early demise. She crossed the room to the edge of the bed and turned on a softly glowing table lamp. After reading her name and address typed carefully on the front yet again, she worked the frayed seal open once more to withdraw the contents.

Though she had gone over everything a dozen times, she still didn't fully comprehend the words on the paperwork. She reached for the letter first, and held it briefly against her chest.

"I wish this really were for me, and not a mistake," she said out loud in the quiet room.

The paper was thick and yellowed with age, and honestly looked far too old to be applied to her, but they had sent it anyway. She laughed a little to herself, because she didn't even know who "they" were. Silently, she read from the page.

> *My dearest Jasmine,*
>
> *I had hoped to find my way to you one day, and to make everything right that was put wrong in your past. Please know that although I never reached you in your time here, I did everything I could for you.*
>
> *You must follow your heart—for the answers you seek may save us all yet. That is all I can tell you without raising alarm, but know that I have always loved you, my child, and every day that has passed for me lives bright with your memory.*
>
> *Trust and Believe.*

Included with the letter was a deed that illustrated the ownership of a piece of property on Rue Royal. While it was in her name and detailed her address in California exactly, the title was signed by a clerk and dated over one hundred years ago.

"Maybe nobody will notice," she said to herself with a hint of sweet sarcasm. The last item inside the envelope was a heavy brass key. She weighed it in her hand, like maybe the feel of it could give her some kind of clue. There was only one way to find out how real this letter was, and she knew what she had to do.

Late summer was making its last stand in the Crescent City and Jasmine pulled on a pair comfortable, stone washed jeans and a long-sleeved white T-shirt. The nights would do their best to hang on to the last sultry remnants of southern heat, but the Mississippi River would have its way with the town and roll out the tendrils of damp, chill air that haunted the back alleys and narrow passages as they wound their ancient ways throughout the city.

She glanced briefly into the mirror above the dresser, more out of habit than anything else, as she swept her dark hair on top of her head with the ease of practice. Her green eyes widened as she was captured by an intense moment of déjà vu. A brief look around the room reassured her that this was a new place and she had nothing to worry about. Still, the feeling was difficult to shake and she kept looking over her shoulder as she rode the elevator down into the well-lit lobby of her hotel.

She blinked a little against the stark lights, and marveled at the amount of activity in the hotel so late in the evening. The buttery, cream colored floor shined as she made her silent way across the marble surface. Lush red and gold velvet couches decorated the area, and even at this hour, people were lounging on them, drinking and laughing with the ease brought on by their circle of friendship.

Jasmine set her hand on the cold brass door plate and prepared to push it outward. With an almost wistful gaze, she looked over shoulder once more at the people in the lobby. They all seemed so happy, so beautiful, all decked out in their party dresses and suits. Almost everyone had their arm around someone they loved and she felt a moment of longing. That feeling she was never quite where she belonged pushed to the forefront of her thoughts, and the darkness past the door beckoned her with almost comforting solitude.

The map she had studied on the plane seemed so one-dimensional now that she was faced with the actual brick-laid streets and broken-slate sidewalks of the town. She crossed Canal, carefully stepping over the street car rails that ran throughout the famous city.

The Quarter swallowed her whole as she walked the edge to Rue Royal. She felt a connection to this strange place, this world that still believed in magic and dreams.

The street lights were fairly dim as well as few and far between, but that didn't lend her a feeling of danger like it should have. It only served to heighten her sense of anonymity as she slipped between the pools of radiance with the thought this might be her only chance to see the place on the deed–before the morning came and alerted "them" to the mistake they had made by sending her the package.

All the buildings she passed by were closed up tight for the evening, but enticing, mysterious looking objects glittered in the display windows like rare treasures. Most all of the doors were at least partially glass and had their street number prominently displayed in gilded paint. She knew she was getting close to the address she'd penciled in on the front of the envelope, and a nervous feeling began to settle in the pit of her stomach. The key felt extremely heavy inside the package, and pulled at her, though she knew it was just her imagination.

With a steadying breath, she counted the next number and arrived at the place her answers should have been. Instead, there was a gap in the sequence and her destination was not there.

She looked at the two buildings in front of her. Hard brick and time-washed wood made up the front of the flat styled antique shops that had been labeled with the street numbers. She considered that the document could have been made in error, or even that the numbers might have changed over the past century and the place simply didn't exist anymore.

She stood there, lost in thought and battling the grave disappointment of losing a chance to find out about her past, when he approached as silent as the night.

The delicate hair on the back of her neck began to rise and her skin was suddenly alive with an electric chill. The feeling was very much like the sensation she experienced with her reoccurring dream—a slight hint of displacement or a shift of her senses.

From instinct alone, Jasmine took a step backward as he neared. She felt confident she could defend herself in most situations and had every intention of doing just that if he made any threatening moves. Sensing her tension, he stopped a good distance away and regarded her with an intensity she found somewhat unsettling.

Raising her chin as a sign of strength, she boldly looked him over as she squared her shoulders.

"I apologize if I have startled you, Miss." He smiled at her, and his tone was so friendly that she wondered if she had misread the strange look in his eyes just a moment before. His demeanor became so casual and his regard for her turned immediately flattering. Her shoulders relaxed, and she realized she had been holding her breath.

Just some guy coming in from the bar, she told herself, feeling a bit silly for her initial guarded reaction.

"No, I am sorry, actually." She felt more at ease as the stranger slipped his hands into his pants pockets and rocked back on his heels. "Not that I'm trying to appear the damsel in distress or anything, but I was looking for a street number that doesn't seem to exist at the moment."

He raised an eyebrow at her statement, but his face was a mask of polite interest only. With a nearly unnoticeable step in her direction, he carefully held out his hand and waited for her to pass him the envelope that clearly had a set of numbers scrawled across the front.

"Ah, my knight in shining armor after all," she said lightly, but looked directly into his deep amber eyes. He had finely sculpted features, a strong jaw, full lips and high cheekbones half hidden beneath his light brown hair.

"I'm Lucas," he said a little shyly, and smiled at her as he brushed the stray strands of hair away from his face.

Jasmine took the last step closer and stood next to him under the street lamp. She was unwilling to part with the envelope, even to place it in the hands of her new friend for directions, so she held it up where the illumination from the feeble overhead light reflected off the yellowed surface. He gently placed his fingertips against the edge as if to steady the offering, but when he read her writing his hand trembled violently.

She immediately glanced up at his face in alarm, but he was perfectly composed and looked as totally innocent as he did a few moments ago.

"That was quite a cool breeze," he said, shaking slightly and rubbing his arms briskly with his hands.

"I suppose it was," she answered him, not sure if she had felt the chill, which must surely have passed them by as he stood shivering before her.

"Anyway, this seems to be my lucky day." He smiled at her in the most charming manner. If she had just passed him on the street, he would have struck her as an eager college boy who just got invited to an all-night party with free beer and hot wings.

"That depends on what you consider lucky," she said sweetly and crossed her arms over her chest with a stubborn look.

"You see," he explained and leaned towards her with a conspiratorial look, "a beautiful young woman just moved into my neighborhood and I know exactly which building she lives in."

"Oh really?" she replied coolly with the raise of an eyebrow. "I'm pretty sure I can't see how you're going to get lucky from that."

He gave her a look of surprise before his handsome features released a stunning smile. She had no doubt he had little trouble swaying the young female tourists around town, but she was not so easily flattered. Jasmine always had her share of attention from any number of men who made no attempt to hide their admiration for her beauty. None of that mattered, because she had never found a person who matched her soul or stirred feelings of love deep inside; and it would take more than a few clever lines from this attractive young man to sway her affections.

Though her eyes swept appreciatively over his sleek and muscular form as he strolled a few feet away from the streetlight, she was unable to feel anything more than a fondness for this stranger. With his back to her, he slipped a key from his pocket and unlocked a tiny wooden door that she assumed must have gated an alley between the two buildings.

"They just replaced the iron grate a few years before, so anyone who hasn't been along for a while wouldn't have a key, of course." He looked over his shoulder, nodding for her to follow him. When she didn't come immediately, he tossed her smile of reassurance and went through on his own.

Hoping not too many axe murderers had keys to the alleyways where damsels in distress needed to go, she followed his lead. The stone walls were impossibly close, and glistened damply in the rapidly disappearing light behind her. Lucas had already gone to the end of the passage and she could see his shadow just outside the exit. With fast fingers, she smoothed her dark, curly hair; it always had a tendency to frizz in wet weather, and this damp, chilly city was giving it the opportunity of a lifetime to misbehave.

The tight walkway gave way to a spacious, intimately lit courtyard. She had heard New Orleans was famous for its little hidden gardens of paradise, but it still amazed her that something so beautiful could be contained behind a nondescript door surrounded by decrepit buildings.

"This is amazing," she said, looking at the old shop fronts that lined the small, private square. A second story topped the tall glass windows of the buildings, with wrought iron balconies just dripping with green, vibrant ferns. Some of the iron work was beautifully intricate, and soft lights hung over many of the edges.

"The Quarter is a relatively small place," her new friend explained, seeing that she had never encountered a setup like this before. "There are a lot of spots like this with old shops off crowded streets. Almost always the owners live above, but since Hurricane Katrina, even some of these ancient store spaces below have been turned into living quarters."

He gestured to a small alcove with well placed lights in the front display window. "This is me."

Jasmine wandered in the direction he indicated and saw what must have been a very exclusive art gallery. The paintings in the window were so exquisite, so expertly done that she had a hard time believing these were not prints from some famous museum. They evoked so many feelings inside her, but she felt the most like she was looking at oceans of time with countless heartbreaks and innumerable joys.

He carefully studied her reaction, measuring her character maybe, and she finally turned to look at him.

"So, this is you?" She indicated the balcony above the gallery, and he gave her another one of his award winning smiles, but his eyes seemed haunted for a moment in the shadows.

"These are all mine, the paintings." He nodded at her look of surprise. "But I do actually live upstairs, if that is what you mean."

"Okay. This is me, then."

She peered in the direction of the address and into the darkest, most secluded corner of the courtyard, which housed her place.

"Of course," she muttered to herself, pulling the heavy brass key from its hiding place and advancing into the shadows. It was only a moment before Lucas was at her side with a flashlight, though the darkness seemed to have a life of its own and retreat wasn't much of an option as it engulfed the luminous stream.

"Might need new batteries for that thing," she said sourly, not wanting to appear ungrateful, but the dim light he offered did very little to cut through the heavy blackness that seemed to drape over the doorway. She could make out the keyhole, and with a moment of apprehension, she stuck the antique brass relic inside. The second she turned the end of the key, Lucas' light went completely dark. He muttered a few powerful and archaic curses under his breath.

Jasmine turned to regard his language choice with surprise.

"You cuss like a sailor." She laughed a little uneasily. "But, like a sailor on Sinbad's ship a handful of centuries ago."

"I apologize, my lady." He bowed in an old court fashion, and she laughed out loud at his display as he continued in almost the same breath. "May I invite you to dinner tomorrow evening? We're having energizer bunny."

"I try not to eat anything that keeps going and going and going—if you know what I mean."

"That would be most of the cuisine in New Orleans, I fear." He sighed in mock disappointment. "Wait here a moment, though. I'll be right back."

Standing alone with her key turned in the door, her eyes began to adjust a little, and Jasmine had to face the realization that answers to her past could very well lie inside.

Lucas certainly was a distraction she hadn't expected, but she couldn't resist turning the knob and pushing the door open before he came back. It opened easily, though she had envisioned rusty hinges and an alarming squeak that would rouse the rest of her new neighbors for sure. Flakes of dark green paint that hadn't been disturbed for ages fluttered down to her feet in the courtyard light just as Lucas returned with an oil lamp. She hurriedly slipped the key into her pocket in order to accept his offering.

"We all have a lot of these after the hurricane," he said as he handed her a glass lantern filled with red liquid. The chimney was already beginning to blacken from the smoke, but she was grateful for the light. The flame struggled to penetrate the darkness in the way the flashlight had, but it didn't go out. With a lot of courage, she stepped inside the threshold and onto what looked like very dusty, blonde hardwood floor stripping. With an excited gesture, she turned to motion Lucas inside. He immediately made a move to follow her, but as he neared the threshold, he came up short. It was almost as if he changed his mind at the last minute as he backed away uncertainly.

"Actually," he said quickly, "I have to go check on something over at the store, with your permission."

He looked so uncomfortable that she merely nodded. He immediately turned to leave.

"Men," she said under her breath. "So dependable."

With careful fingers, she turned the wick higher and increased the light emanating from the lantern. What she saw shocked her to the very core.

Chapter Two

It looked exactly like her. Jasmine crept closer to the painting on the wall to examine the portrait. It was hung inside an elaborate and gilded frame, but no glass covered the front. Somewhere in the back of her mind she knew it had been done with oils and nothing could enclose that kind of paint or it would ruin.

"Yay for fourth grade art class," she said to herself as she began to gently blow a layer of dust off the picture. She didn't dare touch it; she had no idea how old it was or what would happen if she did.

The woman who posed for the work was dressed in some type of medieval gown, but not any couture that she was associated with. The artistic style itself seemed hauntingly familiar, and as a history teacher, she thought she should be able to place the time frame of the painting, but the before-mentioned fourth grade art class was long past and she couldn't think of the period or artist.

The uncanny likeness of the portrait set her on edge, and she peered carefully around the rest of the room. There were a few antique looking chairs and one small settee, not unlike the one she saw earlier in the hotel, though the color was impossible to discern through the layers of dust that coated everything. It could have easily been a reading room, with small tables placed near the seats and partially burned candlesticks that looked like they had waited forever to be set alight once more.

She walked to one small, round table near the closed doorway into the next room. The candle there had obviously burned the lowest, and she saw a small book lying next to it.

Jasmine carefully put the oil lamp down and picked up the surprisingly heavy volume, leaving the envelope in its place. Her hands tingled slightly as she gently brushed the dust from the cover. The book was leather bound, stiff from age and disuse. She ran her fingertips over the front and felt the intricate designs worked into the cover. Slowly, she opened the book, anxious to see what such a lovely binding could hold.

The paper was thick and smelled musty as she turned the pages. Much to her disappointment, the ink had faded to almost nothing. She could barely make out any words, just a few here and there as she strained to see in the lamp light.

Perhaps later, in the daytime ... she told herself, reluctant to set the book back in its place. It seemed to her as if it had an important story to tell, one that she just had to know.

With the lamp back in her hand, she held the light high above her head in the hopes that the illumination might reveal something as clever as a light switch.

"Note to self," she said out loud in the room. "Remember to call electrician in the morning." With that thought in mind, she pulled out her cell phone and flipped it open. It was still turned off from her flight and she had completely forgotten to power it back on. The screen glowed with its vibrant, reassuring light as the phone started up, but no connection bars were available at all.

I suppose the Internet is probably out of the question. She kept her thoughts to herself this time, humorously thinking the shop shouldn't be made aware of the twenty-first century progress she was planning. Slipping the phone back into her shoulder bag, she put her hand on the door knob to the next room and pushed it open.

She stared in awe, spinning around the large area she had just entered. Shelves lined the walls on all four sides, from floor to ceiling and they were filled with books of every shape and size. A ladder stretched to the top and she saw a tiny catwalk near the upper section where someone might go around and look at the books on the highest level.

Her arm began to ache from holding the lamp over her head for so long, and she dropped it to her side to let it hang for a moment. That was when she noticed the footprints in the dust. She immediately held her breath, and saw that they trailed across the floor to a shadowy door on the far side of the spacious room.

Carefully, without disturbing the rest of the coating that

blanketed the wood, she stepped into each print in succession, matching every step perfectly. Before she really had a plan, she was at the door and going through it.

She was immediately bathed in moonlight as she stepped through into another courtyard, much smaller than the one that supported the shops out front, but very beautiful in a decaying, ancient way. Two marble benches sat on either side of the small opening, and matching stone angels crumbled silent tears through their eroded hands next to each one. The only thing that seemed alive was a persistent vine, and then she smelled the fragrant blossoms that twisted their way over the stone.

"The flowers," she whispered out loud, her heart beating fast. She closed her eyes and instantly a flash of the dream came before her vision ...

Falling stones, fire and the screams of women echoed in her ears as she ran through the corridors of the castle. But she was not alone. Someone held her hand tight and she clenched her fist.

She abruptly shook her head and opened her eyes wide. She had a lot of experience dealing with the dream over the years, and while it might have never been as strong as it was now, she had learned to be stronger and she knew how to control it. With her mind cleared, she looked around once more and finished her examination. There was a fountain in the middle, but it was bone dry and the stone tiers in the center had collapsed ages ago. The bottom basin was littered with leaves and debris, but the blooming vine circled it, alive with the sweetest scent she had ever encountered.

This is my place. She smiled to herself, completely unafraid. The footprints in the dust were forgotten and she stood quietly in the moonlight, feeling more at home than she ever had before.

A gentle but persistent tapping noise interrupted her reverie, and she was forced back into reality a little unwillingly. The sound was definitely coming from the front of the bookstore and with a curious smile on her face she picked up her light and went to discover the source.

He leaned against the frame of the doorway just outside, and a warm light from the courtyard lit his hair like a halo, though his features and intentions were shrouded by the shadows. Clasped within the slender, artistic fingers of one hand were two fine crystal glasses that sparkled with a burst of prismatic light against the brick. The other held a bottle of wine, which he lightly tapped against the peeling green wood around the door.

She approached him quite closely in the dark confinement of the doorway and turned the wick of her lamp all the way down. She wondered if he could see the expression on her face in the absolute darkness of the foyer, and purposefully came within inches of him. His scent was clean and musky, and she thought she could make out the corners of his mouth, turned upward.

"What have we here?" she inquired playfully, leaning a little to her right to look outside. The flame from maybe a dozen candles cast the outer courtyard in a very appealing light, and she noticed a white cloth on a table in the center with an ice bucket sitting on top.

"I thought I could perhaps lure my lovely new friend into a central location where she might feel safe enough to have a glass of wine with me." He took a few steps back and she was able to see the intensity in his eyes again. More controlled than before, but it was still there. She felt a flag of caution go up, but he seemed harmless enough in his cable knit sweater and jeans.

"I don't usually accept drinks from strangers." She raised an eyebrow, preparing to judge his reaction.

"But there's cheese whiz and crackers," he exclaimed with mock surprise, and they both laughed together.

Jasmine regarded his easy manner and once again let her feelings pass. She really was quite hungry and it would be a terrible shame to waste a bottle of wine.

"Alright, I'll let you lure me a little bit. But that's all. Only a small amount of luring with a new friendship is permitted."

"I am honored," he said simply, and his tone was very sincere. Feeling a little more comfortable, she let him guide her to the table and pour the wine. After he took the first drink, she relaxed. She knew dawn would be here soon, shedding light on a mystery that was all hers to explore. But right now there was this sweet, warm darkness and handsome company.

"How long have you lived here, Lucas?" she eventually asked after he had nearly consumed an entire glass of wine without saying a word. Though silent during that time, he had watched her very closely as she took a few occasional sips. Her smallest movement seemed to interest him, and she was feeling a little bit like a lab experiment.

He finally smiled and sat back in his chair. With his artist's fingers, he lightly stroked the rim of his glass as he answered.

"I have been living here for ages, though I feel I have been waiting ages to live here," he answered her cryptically.

This is getting interesting, she thought, sitting up a little straighter.

"Let me guess ... Socrates? Descartes? I'm a little rusty on my philosophy, but if you give me a hint, I think I can get it."

He laughed and waved his hand dismissively. "Then it is my greatest wish that you will someday, as you put it ... get it."

"No clues, huh." She pursed her lips together, wracking her brain to think of the source. "So you want to play rough. Just give me some time and I'm sure I'll have an answer."

"That, my dear Jasmine is something I will be able to give you."

"I didn't tell you my name." The mood completely changed between them in that instant.

His eyes narrowed almost imperceptibly, but she caught it before he caught himself.

"Yes, of course you didn't tell me your name." He took a breath and looked her squarely in the eyes. "It was typed on the outside of the envelope where you wrote this address. I apologize if I have upset you by using it before you introduced yourself to me."

His voice adopted a lilting and teasing tone as he picked up the bottle and refilled his glass with apparent ease. She was immediately reminded that although he had indeed introduced himself to her at almost the moment they met, she had neglected to do the same. She struggled between feelings of guilt for her behavior and the unease of too many coincidences.

"If it's alright with you, I think I'm going to go back inside. It's pretty late and I lost track of the time."

"I don't suppose I could convince you otherwise?" he responded hesitantly, as if he hadn't expected things to turn out this way and didn't have a plan.

"No." She shook her head firmly in a manner he couldn't argue with. "I'm out."

"Very well, then," he said, once more the gentleman. "Allow me to escort you to your door?" With a fluid movement he rose from his chair and offered her his arm.

"Certainly," she said, and hooked her right hand in. He tensed unexpectedly at her touch and she looked up into his face. He seemed a little surprised himself and eased up a bit.

"I guess I don't know my own strength," he joked and took her the few short steps across the courtyard. Without a word he picked up the oil lamp from the outside step where she had deposited it and lit it for her with a nearby candlestick.

"Thanks for everything, Lucas." She smiled, and was truly grateful for all the help he had given her. With a quick movement, she leaned forward and gave him a quick peck on the cheek.

He regarded her with wonder as she stepped backwards into the store.

"I'll always remember the kindness of the first person I met in New Orleans," she teased, and closed the shop door behind her.

"You will remember me well, my beautiful Jasmine," he whispered, as the dirty glass on the windows and door filtered her retreating light within to almost nothing. "Because now, you have met me first."

Lucas had no idea how wrong he really was.

Chapter Three

With a smile still on her face, she went to the small table and made a half-hearted effort to brush the layers of dust off the accompanying chair. The small amount of wine seemed like a lot combined with her lack of sleep and the wearing excitement of finding this place.

The oil lamp began to smoke again almost immediately, and she pushed it to the edge to try to avoid the black fumes. She reached for the leather bound book once more, and worked her fingertips across the surface to remove as much ancient coating as possible. It looked like it had all been hand tooled, but the details were so perfect and fine. She was able to make out an elaborate design on the cover, which looked very much like the icon for infinity, interwoven with beautiful markings that she was unable to read.

Her eyes strained to see more, and she was sure the dust wasn't helping them either. She was just trying to decide whether she should go back to the hotel and return in the morning or tough it out on the aged settee, when she first heard the noise.

It started out softly, but became a very insistent sound of trickling water and she rose from her chair in concern, imagining somehow her intrusion into this place after so many years could have caused a water pipe or something to burst.

"Think on the bright side," she told herself out loud to push back the unwelcome vision of ancient, wet books in the other room. "This could very well mean we have a bathroom in the place!"

Completely distracted, she slipped the book into her shoulder bag and picked up the lamp. At the very least, she could hit someone over the head with it if she had to.

Eyes squeezed closed, she pushed the door into the book area open, preparing to see anything from water dripping off the ceiling to a pool on the floor ruining the books on the lower shelf. With one eye cautiously open to survey the situation, she was relieved to see that there was no water damage in sight. Something seemed terribly out of place in the room, but it was nothing she could put her finger on at the moment. It hung at the back of her mind as something out of sync, but before she could spend much time thinking about it, the sound of running water hit her full on and it was obviously coming from the courtyard.

In a near panic, she swiftly crossed the room with no other thought in mind than to go through the door at the far end. Her quick footsteps stirred up little dust devils, and it never occurred to her that her shoes left a trail of foot prints all the way across the perfectly undisturbed coat of dust on the floor boards.

There was water in the fountain. And not only was there water in the fountain, all the stone tiers that had lain in a decaying heap just an hour ago were up and about, looking pretty solid and functional as the water bubbled over their rims.

"I probably didn't even have a whole glass of wine, you know," Jasmine announced to the illusion in front of her. "So, you can just stop it now."

She crossed her arms and waited, but her courtyard still appeared to be operating under the premise that it was functioning normally. She briefly considered going back out to have Lucas come take a look, before she realized she must be dreaming.

I feel asleep at the table, of course, she thought with some relief, and hoped she wasn't too uncomfortable back there with the oil lamp smoking away. If she had learned any life lesson by now, it was that dreams can seem very real, even when they are not. Still, she was glad she had the sleep inspired version of the lantern with her when she heard the heavy groan that issued from the far side of the fountain.

She covered the short distance with a few fast footsteps. The fountain had obstructed her view of only a small part of the courtyard, but in that part laid the huddled figure of a man. He was dressed a bit strangely, his clothing almost all soft brown leather. She noticed in an offhand way that none of what he wore had zippers or buttons, and it all seemed to tie or tuck together in some manner.

His desperate gasp brought her out of her remote analysis, and forgetting this was a dream, she knelt beside him immediately. With strong, but gentle hands, she rolled him from his side and onto his back.

They very moment Jasmine saw his face, time all around her seemed to slow to a crawl and her heart beat leaped alarmingly. A sweeping feeling of wonder shot through her veins and her soul felt like it had finally come home to stay.

In that instant his hands shot out and clasped her neck, immediately cutting off her airflow. His thickly lashed eyelids flew open as he made the contact and she helplessly watched his beautiful blue eyes clear and form some kind of recognition as he held her powerfully over him.

He let go of her almost as soon as he had grabbed her, but she remained just inches above him, transfixed by the reverent look on his face.

"Please forgive me, my Lady," he spoke in the smallest whisper, but his voice was deep and beautiful. The sound of it made her heart flutter again for just a moment and though he hadn't really injured her in any way, she felt lightheaded just the same. His hand raised once more, but slowly this time, and he brushed his fingertips against her cheek with a caress that stirred more emotion inside her than she had even been able to imagine in the whole of her life.

The slightest corner of his mouth turned up in what had to be a smile and Jasmine immediately felt she was in far worse shape than this unbelievably gorgeous man lying in her courtyard at the moment; but the light in his eyes faded quickly and his hand dropped from her skin.

Her face tingled where he had lightly grazed it and she felt as if some small part of her heart had been peeled back when his hand fell away from her.

"Hey ... you." She gently patted his cheek, waiting to see if it would rouse him. Dawn was cresting the top of the buildings, lending her a little more light than the lamp was casting even just a short minute ago.

His pallor was alarmingly waxy and his breath more shallow than it was before he had expended all his energy trying to needlessly defend against her.

"We're going to have to get you up." She slipped an arm beneath his neck and shoulders, thankful for all the nights she spent at the gym picking up heavy weights for what had seemed like no apparent reason at the time.

The stranger staggered to his feet a little unsteadily, but she was able to hold him. He winced when he came to fully stand, and his eyes opened once again. With him upright, she could see he was well over six feet tall, and ducked underneath his arm to support him.

His breath was uneven, and Jasmine turned her face upward to gauge his awareness. To her surprise, he was looking back at her, his eyes wide.

"My God," he breathed into the still air of the morning. "You're beautiful."

Jasmine felt the raw honesty of his tone and there was no mistaking the awe he held for her on his face. Outwardly, she felt so small next to this stately figure of a man, but on the inside she soared on a pedestal well above the likes of all the mortals she had envied in her lifetime.

"I hope you didn't hit your head," she responded with a slight blush, but he was already slumping in her grasp. "Rest here for a minute." Jasmine guided him to the lower rim of the fountain and began to sit him on the edge. "I'll go grab a doctor and we'll get you all fixed up."

"No!" He came fully alive at that moment, struggling against her. "I cannot leave this place now."

"You aren't leaving," she assured him, thinking he wasn't going anywhere until she got to know him better, even if he was crazy.

"We can't touch the ring while it's still active." He pushed at her desperately in an effort to get away.

"What ring?" She stopped for a moment, trying to understand his words as she quit pushing him down.

His grasped at her with a last struggling pull and both of them tumbled against the fountain. She knocked hard into it first, and heard a grinding noise like stone turning against stone. His arm went protectively around her waist immediately and they both splashed into the water …

•

The ground was hard and covered in leaves as they cascaded together in a small heap at the foot of an impressive pile of broken stones.

Jasmine lifted her herself up and saw a beautiful forest of fall colored trees surrounding the clearing where she and her new fairy tale friend had landed.

"Ok," she said to herself. "Maybe I hit my head instead."

A quick glance around the area let her know that they were nowhere near the book shop, or probably New Orleans for that matter, as she regarded the majestic Blue Mountains in the background.

She bent over her unconscious companion with a crazy smile.

"Do you mind telling me where we are?"

When he didn't answer, she tapped him on the shoulder. He made a small noise, and rolled onto his side.

She was about to become angry when she saw the red stain on the bright yellow leaves where he had just been laying.

"Oh my God." She knelt and pulled a few rogue leaves from his leather vest. Not only was he bleeding, but his soaked clothing let her know he had been wounded for quite a while.

Out of instinct, she pulled the cell phone from her bag and flipped it open. It searched futilely for a signal and came back with a disappointing beep.

"Can you hear me now?" she quipped in a sarcastic manner as she held the useless phone to her ear.

She looked around at the autumn laden trees with a mountain in the background that was bigger than the one in all of the Paramount Picture movies.

"I'm in big trouble," she stated calmly into her phone before she closed it up and put it in the bag.

She looked around the clearing in an attempt to guess at a possible location. It looked like they might be in some type of garden on the outskirts of a forest, though it was obviously long abandoned. There appeared to be some kind of overgrown path leading away and she thought she could see an open area through the trees in the distance.

"What would Survivorman do?" There were big chunks of stone and lots of fallen branches, but nothing that was going to make her friend very comfortable for the moment.

She knelt on the ground at his back and gently pulled his shirt up. The fact that he barely winced as it peeled away from his skin made her a little nervous. There was a long, deep gash in a diagonal pattern from his right shoulder blade to the middle of his back. She was immediately relieved it didn't look like a puncture wound at all, but if his shirt was any witness to his injuries, he'd lost a lot of blood.

Without thinking, she ran her fingers up the spine of his muscular back, impressed with how perfectly his body was formed. He shivered slightly and she saw his waxy cheeks had taken on a pinkish hue. At first she thought he might be feeling better, but when she touched his forehead she understood he was burning up with fever.

"Alright," she told him, even though she thought he probably couldn't hear her. "I'm going down the path just a little way to see if there is anyone that can help us. You can stay here and keep watch."

After a brief pause assured her he didn't have any complaints about her brilliant plan, she stood and made her way through the woods, carefully listening for anything that might give her a clue anyone was around. The trail went on for just a short length when she began to see emerald green grass through the opening in the distance. She was just beginning to feel encouraged when she heard the sound of heavy crying just beyond the trees.

She instantly froze and listened for any other disturbances. All that came to her on the breeze was a deeply heartfelt sob that sounded distinctly masculine. Breaking through the tree line, she found herself on a rolling hill near the top of a larger series of mountains that looked like they came straight off a post card.

Standing alone in the distance, underneath one single behemoth of an ancient tree, was an old cabin-like structure. The wood on the outside was grey and warped with time and the elements. Part of the front porch had fallen in and it looked very unsafe for any means of habitation.

Jasmine decided to skirt it and have a look on the other side when she heard the devastated cry once again. There was no doubt it was coming from inside the decaying building. Though it seemed like it should still be morning, the sun was sinking behind the higher mountains and casting the low lying hill top in a cool shadow.

She slowly approached the cabin, but no one came out or

challenged her in any way. With careful steps, she lightly placed her foot on the portion of the porch that hadn't fallen to ruin. It creaked predictably under her weight, and she came to stand fully before the rotting door. Just as she raised her hand to knock, a light flared on inside, instantly warming the dingy glass window on the front of the little house.

She was suddenly filled with an unexplained feeling of joy that soared through her very soul, and she felt welcome at once. Exhaling, she tried to dispel what little apprehension remained as she knocked on the bloated, twisted wood. She half expected the door to swing inward, revealing a cozy little dinner party with a happy family seated at a well stocked table. Indeed, even as she waited she was sure she could hear the laugh of a little girl and feet dancing across a sturdy floor.

No one answered. She considered searching the glade beyond the cabin because no one seemed to respond inside, but the thought of the gash along her companions back led her to knock once more. A little angry now from the disregard she was being dealt, she tapped her feet lightly on the worn boards. Looking down in alarm to see if it had any plans to collapse under her, she saw a soft glow through the crack underneath the door.

Clear sounds of laughter and music were coming from the other side of the wood now and Jasmine had about all she could take by that point. With her lips pursed together, she grabbed the latched handle on the door and popped it with her thumb, swinging the crooked planks wide open.

There was nothing inside.

Dry and curled leaves scurried past her feet as the air from the doorway swept through the grey, long abandoned room.

At one time there had been a dinner table, but one of the legs had been chewed through or rotted off; she couldn't be sure which. It tilted in a haphazard manner and a few dull metal plates had made their way to the edge. One or two wooden chairs looked like they were holding together, more or less, and a full sized bed took up a whole corner on the opposite side of the single room dwelling.

A dozen unidentified creatures skittered across the floor as she came in, kicking aside parts of the roof that had fallen through and littered the cabin. She went to the bed and pulled off layers of moth eaten blankets, but in truth everything seemed so old that there wasn't much left for the moths to eat. She was relieved to find a sheet of linen on the very bottom that was dry and musty, but looked completely untouched. The temperature inside was several degrees cooler than without, and she thought they were probably in for a chilly night. Without much to chose from, she knew she had to get that guy off the ground and inside for the evening while she figured out what to do.

Now that she had a little bit of a plan, she felt more in control as she went back to the clearing where she left her friend. He looked so peaceful, almost like he was sleeping on the hard ground .

To her relief, his beautiful blue eyes fluttered open and he looked at her with confusion. She knelt down and pulled his left arm over her shoulder while she wrapped hers carefully around his waist, trying not to come up against his wound. Her cheek pressed against his hot neck, the top of her head under his chin. She could feel the pulse from his jugular against her lips and without realizing what she was doing, Jasmine paused for just a moment to lightly brush them against his throat.

He immediately reacted to her touch and a soft groan escaped his mouth. She was afraid she might have hurt him somehow, when she discovered he was trying to speak.

"We must find it." He struggled between breaths. "We can't leave the ring here."

"I'd like to remind you that last time I touched a ring we fell through a fountain and into—" She paused, assessing their surroundings. "—this unbelievably beautiful and romantic mountainside."

She pulled away, and to her surprise he stayed in a sitting position, looking at her as if she were some kind of heavenly vision.

"I see your point," she said, all about finding rings now, as she searched through the rubble where they'd tumbled out.

"It will be small, perhaps the size of a wristband," he instructed quietly, but his voice was so warm and sensual it sent a shiver down her spine. She saw it then, a shining silver loop as large as a bracelet, propped against one of the moss covered stones. The air seemed to sizzle around it and her fingertips tingled as she reached for the rim, touching it only as much as she needed to pick it up.

Jasmine held the vibrating circlet far out in front of her as she came back to the handsome stranger. He nodded at her like she was handing over the crown jewels and when he touched it, the metal instantly shrank. To her considerable surprise, he slipped it nonchalantly onto his finger.

She let out a cry of alarm, and immediately jumped onto his sitting form, wrapping her arms around his neck, eyes squeezed tightly closed.

Nothing happened for quite a few moments, until he spoke softly into her ear.

"The ring isn't active right now."

"Right," she said flatly, opening her eyes and blushing as she found herself on his lap. Her lips were just a few short inches from his mouth and she was acutely aware of a hot ache deep inside that begged her to press her body against his hard chest.

His breathing was fast now, and ignoring his injuries he slowly slid his strong hands around the small of her back, running his fingers up her spine.

Jasmine drew in a sharp breath at his sure and steady touch, her back arching automatically as he traced what felt like her very soul along her back. She'd never experienced such a ravenous need to breathe in someone else's breath. The desire to be as near to him as possible felt so natural, so necessary, that she thought the world could end right then and there if they couldn't come together and blend their hearts at that very moment.

Without thinking, her hands began to caress his neck, stretching down his back as she leaned closer. His involuntary cry of pain brought her senses back on track and with wide eyes, she sprang from his lap. The color drained from his face and his jaw was clenched tight against the physical onslaught. He began to let himself down easily onto the bright bed of leaves once more and she was afraid if he got all the way down she wouldn't be able to get him up if she didn't do something fast.

"I have a feeling you're the only person I know in the neighborhood, so let's get you inside before it gets dark and we have to fend off werewolves and fairies and God only knows what else lives on the other side of a fountain."

Jasmine got him to his feet and though he seemed unaware of his surroundings, he still was able to follow her lead and make it down the path without stumbling.

There was no denying the fact that the air was growing rapidly cooler.

"Bring it on," Jasmine whispered to the shadows that grew in length right before her eyes as they made it to the open grass. The cabin looked exactly as it had before, and now that she knew there weren't going to be any surprises, she made for it as swiftly as she could with the extra weight across her shoulders.

It was a little difficult to maneuver him onto the porch, and the warped planks groaned threateningly under the weight of two people. Just as she was trying to figure out a way to slip one of her hands free and pop the latch again, the door swung open on its own.

"I'm really handling all this very well, I'd say," she said flatly, as she took advantage of the eerie situation to get him through the doorway. Without a struggle, she laid him face down on the old bed.

"I never thought I'd say this," she chatted conversationally to her unresponsive companion, "but I think we need to get you out of these clothes."

She knelt gently on the bed next to him, and slowly peeled his shirt away from his back before she slid her hands underneath to get the front raised. His stomach was rock hard, even in his semi conscious state. Her fingers lingered on his hot skin as she lightly brushed his strong arms with the soft leather tunic to get it over his head. A mane of dark blonde hair fell slightly past his shoulders, and lay against his tanned back just above the wound.

Jasmine put her face very near his to gauge his breathing, and was totally overwhelmed by his handsome features. His jaw line was square and smooth, with the fullest, sweetest looking lips she had ever seen on a man. His eyes were closed but he had a thick veil of dark eyelashes that she knew framed deep blue eyes.

"I don't know who you're," she whispered intimately to him, "and I'm probably in a straightjacket somewhere filling up with meds. But if I had my druthers, I could think of nowhere else I'd rather be than here in this old cabin with you."

She reached out to stroke his hair and heard a light step behind her. Already nervous, she sprang from the bed and spun around. No one was there and she was reminded that the light was quickly getting dimmer in the small space.

"Okay, I'm all for it not getting dark in here tonight when the sun goes down. Anyone else?" She raised her hand and looked around for some kind of light source. There was a fireplace at the far end of the room, though various stones had fallen from it and lay around the opening in a haphazard fashion. She stepped over them and got down on the floorboards to have a look. The chimney seemed clear, with no nests or fallen branches inside. At the very moment her head was shoved up in the flue, she distinctly heard the sound of a little girl's laughter out front.

Hoping to catch the culprit this time, she jumped to her feet and got out onto the porch as quickly as possible. Dew was beginning to form on the pristine emerald grass and it was obvious it hadn't been disturbed since their passing left a trail away from the clearing. Trying to move as quietly as possible, she stepped off the creaking timber and into the yard, so she wouldn't make a sound when she went behind the building.

Her heart was pounding at the thought they weren't alone, but she didn't know if it was from relief or fear. She rounded the corner and hadn't realized she was holding her breath until she saw an empty garden and a sigh escaped her lips.

Most of the vegetation had seeded and blown away, but she saw an old rusty pump handle poking up just over the top of a brown patch of stalks. She walked over to it and studied the mechanism. It looked like every other pump she had come across on an old farm in the last fifty years.

So, Jasmine thought, *this one makes the second one I've ever seen.*

Completely fascinated by the prospect of running water, she had forgotten the laughter and the reason she came out back to start with. The handle was easy to lift, but pushing it down was far more difficult. Once she got a few pumps off, there was a deep, sinister groan underneath the ground. She immediately released the handle and stepped away, which turned out to be a good idea because just seconds later a huge flow of brown water gushed from the spout. It slowed to a trickle, and she stepped around the saturated earth to try it again. This time the water came out clear and she ran her fingers under the cool flow.

She turned about with thoughts of heading into the cabin to

find some type of container that wouldn't be too filthy when she saw the woodpile stacked up against the back of the cabin.

"Now that's convenient, thanks," she said out loud, in case whatever was making her life easier might find its way clear to drop a roasted chicken on the dilapidated table inside. Upon closer inspection, the pile had been there so long it was as dry and light as driftwood, and it would surely be eager to burn. She took a few of the larger pieces and walked around to the front. It looked like there was a light in the window again, the same as before, and she even had that strange feeling of happiness, followed by regret.

This time was different, though. This time there was a pretty amazing guy inside who needed her help and she didn't intend to let him down. She jumped onto the porch, mindless of the unstable structure, and went to the grimy glass that sat in the small front window. She tried hard to be angry or suspicious as she attempted to look through the layers of dirt but she could only feel a kind of warmth and joy that seemed to belong to someone else.

Almost ashamed of intruding, she went through the front door. Just as she had left it, the room was gloomy inside and he was totally alone, asleep and shivering with his shirt off. Waves of heat radiated off him but he didn't break a sweat. Jasmine knew this was bad and she threw the dried wood into the fireplace, quickly gathering the small sticks and leaves that had cured for many seasons on the floor of the cabin. She made a small bed of kindling in the center and lit it with the book of matches they gave her at the airport when she bought her map. It didn't need any encouragement and the dry tinder burst into flame with a tiny roar.

Jasmine looked around the room, amazed at the difference a warm fire made in terms of light and comfort. It almost felt cozy and inviting inside and she decided to get as much wood in as she could carry before nightfall. Passing the table on her way out, she thought she noticed the dull metal gleam of a large bowl underneath.

"This seems to be my lucky day." She quoted the very same words Lucas used just hours ago.

•

Once she filled the bowl with water, she realized there was no way to hang the pot over the fire, so she tucked it in the corner near the glowing orange coal bed and hoped that would bring it to a boil. She piled on a fresh round of the dry wood from out back just to make sure and in no time at all, the water was bubbling away.

One short look around the small structure let her know there was nothing she could use to clean the nasty looking gouge on her companion's back, so she slipped off her white T-shirt and ripped the bottom off, all the way around.

"It was too long, anyway." She sighed as she tugged the more revealing version back over her head.

With one end of the extra material held over the miniature cauldron, she dipped the fabric into the water and brought it back out. The cloth steamed furiously in the firelight, and she waved it back and forth for a minute until she felt it wouldn't burn him.

Her hands were warm, but when she placed them on his forehead, it was hotter. She stood by the bedside for just one moment as she regarded him. Her heart felt like it was in a vice, she was so overwhelmed by his presence. Even in his condition he radiated such a strong, noble character that she was inexplicably attracted.

As lightly as she could, Jasmine laid the tepid, wet cloth along the jagged mark on his back, hoping that the steam would loosen some of the dried blood and allow her to take care of the wound when she could see it better.

The raging flames from the fireplace played across his tanned back, his muscles deeply highlighted by the shadows they generated. She glanced down at the supple leather pants that fitted his lower form perfectly, sculpted to his thighs like a second skin.

Almost like a child putting her hand into the forbidden cookie jar, she slowly reached out and touched the leather on his hips. It was soft and pliable from the heat of his body and she ran her palm down to his strong upper thigh.

Though Jasmine was a beautiful woman, she didn't have a lot of experience when it came to the seduction of a man. She'd never encountered anyone who drove her to the depths of passion she was just now beginning to realize. Her cheeks flamed as brightly as the fire and her heart pounded in her chest as she stole a look at her sleeping patient.

He was casually staring at her, his eyelids heavy and half open in a manner that veiled his emotions. His lips were slightly parted and had taken on a deep, red hue. Jasmine swiftly removed her hand

and clasped it behind her back as if nothing had happened, and waited to see if he would talk. After a minute of silent observation, she simply couldn't take it any longer and leaned over him with the pretense of putting her hand on his forehead. She became very concerned by the dry heat coming off him.

"I'm no doctor, but I'm pretty sure you have a fever." She pulled back and walked over to the fireplace where she had left her bag. If there was one thing Jasmine was good at, it was being prepared. She always had a bottle of aspirin in her bag, and usually some sleeping pills, though the latter had always been useless against her nightmares.

With a couple of pills in hand, she crossed back to the bed, trying to think of a way to convince him to take her offering. He watched her walk across the floor, and she felt nervous. Never had it meant so much to her that she was beautiful in someone else's eyes.

"Thank you," he said simply as she came near. He sounded so very tired, but once more his voice sent sensual shivers down her spine and she found herself waiting to see if he would speak even one more word to her again.

Before she could think about water to drink, he rolled from his stomach to side and held out his right hand.

Breathe like a normal person! The thought reverberated through her head, but all she saw was his lean, hard chest in the firelight and he was perfectly sculpted as far down as she could see. With what she considered supreme control, Jasmine steadily put the capsules into his upturned palm. He swallowed them easily and regarded her with fully open eyes now; they were dark blue in their intensity.

With a sigh, he took her hand and brought it to his face. She gently held his cheek, trying not to tremble when he turned his head and caressed her open palm with a tender, reverent kiss. Tendrils of electricity shot through her fingers and into the center of her body.

Her knees no longer seemed willing to support her, and Jasmine ended up on the bed next to him before she could help herself.

His breath was hot on her wrist; it inflamed her pulse and made her aware of every single inch of her body that wasn't touching his.

She glanced up into his face, her green eyes full of desire. The look he gave her was ageless and she realized she had never felt so full of grace as she did when she saw herself reflected in his eyes.

"Forgive me," he breathed as if he could no longer control himself.

With a strong, swift motion, he wrapped his right arm around her slender waist and pulled her up against the length of his body as if he were trying to conform to her every curve.

Jasmine lost control the instant she came up against him. His mouth covered hers with such a demanding force that she felt like she was giving up her soul to his passion and she willingly poured everything she had into his deep kiss.

His right hand found its way to the small of her back and with one swift movement, he pressed her against his thigh and she felt him pulse against her. She gasped at the ache that swelled deep inside her, at the emptiness she never realized she had, that he must fill or she would die.

"Wait," he whispered in a tense voice, and she felt him pull away both mentally and physically. The space between them was small, but it felt like oceans of time that separated them.

"I cannot do this to you." His eyes were closed and his jaw line firm with resolution. "I will not dishonor you in this way."

"Um, yes you can." Jasmine was doing her best to keep the edge of panic out of her tone, but didn't think she was doing a very good job. "I really don't mind."

"I don't expect you to understand." He looked at her with a lingering hunger still in his eyes. "My life belongs to my people, my land. I must give everything I have to save them, or we're all lost."

"This is a rotten fairy tale." Jasmine frowned, her body still responding to his closeness in ways she was unable to repress.

"Until my quest is complete, I cannot offer you anything of me. I took you from your world, and I am sorry for that. It was not planned that way, but you saved my life and I could never give you less than you deserve." He watched her carefully as he said this, and she could see he had regained complete control of the situation.

"Alright," she said, and thought about it for a moment. "Then I'll help you save the world, or whatever you have to do, and we can get on with it."

His smile at her comment was reward enough, but when he reached out and lightly stroked her cheek she lost her breath again in an instant.

"Don't you want to go home?" he inquired softly.

"I am home," she said plainly. "Next Tuesday I'm going to the post office to file a change of address."

He gave her a quizzical glance, but pulled her to his chest gently in a protective manner. Jasmine had a little trouble switching gears that easily, but did what she could to get close to him again.

"You can stay with me until we find a way to get you back," he whispered as he kissed the top of her head so lightly she wasn't sure he'd done it.

Though she couldn't have considered sleep just fifteen minutes ago, Jasmine found she was completely exhausted. The fire crackled across the room and it was very warm in the small, enclosed place. She determined to keep her eyes open for about two whole minutes before the comfort of strong arms, combined with the lack of sleep, took her down.

She was afraid the dream was coming; more sure of it than she ever had been before. With a last conscious effort, she entwined her fingers with those of her new companion and prepared to face her demons once more.

Chapter Four

Jasmine held the flower in her tiny hand, crushing it tight as she tried to block out the sounds of chaos and war all around her. She focused on the way it smelled, the bright color of the petals, and it was all she could remember as everything faded.

Her eyes opened in alarm and for a moment she didn't remember where she was. As soon as she tried to sit up, to protect herself, she realized she was still tightly grasping the stranger's fingers. He was well awake and holding her hand as tenderly as possible. Hot tears stained her cheeks and she tried to look away before he could catch a glimpse of them by the faint light of day that was streaming through the window.

"I thought you were asleep," she said with a tremble in her voice. If she had looked his way, she would have seen the compassion on his face and understood she could trust him with her feelings.

"I was," he answered steadily and though he didn't know it, his strong, calm response raised Jasmine's esteem for him by miles. "It's funny, but I thought a light came on and I woke up, though nothing was really there."

"Oh, yeah." She adopted a nonchalant tone, and only her white knuckled grip on his fingers clued him in to her continued vulnerability. "I forgot to tell you. I brought you to a haunted house."

"What do you mean, haunted?" He looked at her directly, and she rewarded him with a smirking glance that let him know she thought he was playing around.

"You know ... Ghosts, spirits, magic, dead people?" Her breathing was returning to normal and she was almost herself again.

"Alright, I know what all that means, but it's obvious to me someone split a time stack here."

"It's good you know what I'm saying, because I have no clue what you're talking about." She released his fingers and stood next to the bed with her hands on her hips.

"All of this is new to you," he began, and she briefly forgot what he was saying as he stood up in front of her. His skin had regained its healthy tone and with no shirt, he was an awesome sight.

"Whoever it was, he was clearly a novice, probably someone trained to fight in the war and so they didn't have the skill of experience." He took a step closer. He had the remnants of her makeshift bandage in his left hand and was studying her newly cropped T-shirt closely.

"It's a rift in time." He shrugged as if his explanation made perfect sense. "The split is healed as well as it can now, but I sense the tear was jagged and messy. Anything you see here are visions of the past, bleeding through the places where it couldn't fully mend."

"Besides wondering if this is even possible, why would someone do something like that?" Jasmine asked. "Where I'm from, if people want to see the past they open a photo album or call up their drunken aunt from last Thanksgiving."

"Every world is different. Here, all of our focus is the study of Time and Space. Where you're from, it could be weapons or medicine. For us, a new dimension in the rift is a sacred place where we study a new world, never interfering. We have seen many things you can never imagine, in many worlds, before or after it has ever happened."

"So it's nothing for you to stumble upon me in a whole different dimension and take me to the dark side?" She was getting a little nervous, mostly because he sounded perfectly reasonable and she was beginning to believe him.

"We're a civilization of Watchers," he answered with patience. "And while parts of our world may seem archaic to you, we might possess technology far greater than your realm has ever seen. We have taken the kindest and best of all we have learned, and shaped our existence by it. But no one has ever come here before. At least, not that I know of."

"Until me." She hesitated, looking to him for answers.

"I don't know everything," he calmly asserted, and gave her a boyish smile that caused her heart beat to speed up.

"Here I am, in the middle of what has to be complete insanity, but all I can do is go along because I have no other choice." She crossed her arms as her stubborn chin came back into play. "So, since we're playing, why did someone split a time stack here?"

"Look around," he said softly, in a manner that instantly made her serious. "There will be a focal point, a place where he began the tear. It may look different than the rest of the cabin, a little younger maybe. We will find our answers there, I suspect. It is no light thing to do what was done at this place. A serious code was broken and no one with the training would do it without leaving a confession."

"A confession?" Jasmine asked, deeply intrigued by the religious symbolism, but he was already across the room and looking intently at the stone around the fireplace.

"Look here." He indicated a small, rectangular rock. When she concentrated on it, it was indeed cleaner and whiter than the others around the fire pit. With great care, he slowly removed the stone to reveal an empty alcove deep inside.

Jasmine sighed in disappointment, but her breath turned into a gasp as her friend reached inside. His entire hand disappeared up to his wrist as he seemed to be feeling around for something. With a nod of satisfaction, he withdrew a small scroll.

She was completely baffled and even a little impressed as he turned to her. The cylinder was a dark white, with gold caps on each end. He popped one off, maybe a little excited himself, and pulled out a small roll of paper.

"Easy … time shift at the focal point. Shall I read it?" he teased, and she was practically jumping up and down with excitement.

He had an adventurous grin on his face as he opened it, but his features took on a dark and sorrowful hue the moment he began to read out loud to her.

My Lord Amarynn,

Please know what I do here today, I do for love. I brought my wife and my daughter to this cabin for love. I left them behind so that I might aid in the holy cause for love …

And I came back after your release to find my family

dead from the shift sickness.

I blame myself, that I didn't see it in them when I smuggled them from the castle after the first attack. If I had left them with the royal entourage as ordered, they might have been saved.

I never knew I had a self serving bone in my body until I took them away and disobeyed command.

And so now I write my confession. I will break my training on this day so that I may catch a glimpse of them one more time, so that I might see them laugh in the sunlight and dance in the glade.

I know the rift will take my soul, but without my wife and child, I have no soul to barter.

Please remember me well.

Malcolm of Ravenswood

Jasmine quietly sat down among the stones in front of the fireplace and gently laid her face in her hands. Finally, a tear would be shed for Malcolm of Ravenswood and his family.

◆

"Are you sure you feel up to this?" Jasmine gave him a sidelong glance as they hiked out of the lower mountains. There was something about him—something so regal and fine. Deep inside, she was afraid when he got where he was going she would lose him to his destiny.

That meant she only had a short amount of time to convince him he needed her in some way. Of course, she knew which way she preferred, but the challenge brought a smile to her lips nonetheless.

"It's a lovely sight." He sighed, looking straight ahead as they strolled through the tall grass. Admittedly, neither one seemed hard pressed to make progress.

Jasmine glanced at their surroundings. The mountains were glorious in their colorful splendor, and she wondered briefly if they were still the mountains of her world, just in another time and space.

"I have always loved this season," she answered him, the smile lingering with her thoughts of ways to win him over.

"As have I." He nodded. "But, what I'm referring to is the look of passion in your green eyes as you smile."

Caught so obviously fantasizing about her companion, Jasmine swiftly turned her face to the side before he could witness the telltale flush of desire on her pale cheeks. She had the soul of a warrior, but the flesh of an innocent and she knew it well.

"Hayden," he whispered softly when her eyes turned away.

"What is that?" Jasmine was so overwhelmed by everything that had happened, and whatever word she didn't understand had the potential to be magical.

"That is my name, beautiful girl," he answered her simply, but his voice went straight to her heart and felt like the familiar caress of an old friend.

"I'm Jasmine." The answer came automatically and Hayden halted his leisurely stride, turning to her with a look of surprise.

"Is that such an unusual name?" she asked him, wondering what there was about her that could cause someone from another world even an ounce of surprise.

"It is an unusual name for a person, but a common name for a flower," he assured her, and it felt like they were both trying as hard as they could not to spook the other with revelations regarding their separate lives.

"I was just saying, Hayden—" She enunciated his name in an exaggerated manner. "That if you weren't sure you felt well enough to travel, we could always stay at the cabin for a day or two until you felt stronger."

His deep blue eyes held her own with a gaze that began as a query, but turned smokey with restrained desire when he saw right through her intentions.

Jasmine broke eye contact once again the moment she realized she had been caught, and cursed herself for feeling so awkward and exposed by a mere man. After all, who was he, anyway? She nudged a stone on the ground with the tip of her shoe in a distracted way, allowing her thick, curly hair to fall over her face and hide her traitorous, flaming cheeks.

She watched his shadow circle the ground and come to rest right in front of her on the wet grass, but she didn't dare look up, suddenly afraid he would be able to see into her soul and glimpse her inexpert affection. As stubborn as the day was young, she crossed her arms over her chest and became quite interested in her damp tennis shoes.

Without a sound, he slipped his hand beneath her veil of hair and firmly lifted her chin with two strong fingers. His free hand brushed her eyes clear of her lustrous mane, and she had no choice but to look at his face. Her breath quickened as the space between them folded into next to nothing and her lips were just inches from his mouth. His hot, rapid breath bathed her skin with warmth and without thinking she licked her lips in anticipation.

A light flared in his eyes like the spark of a thousand suns and he released a long breath.

"Thank you for your concern," he whispered, and his thickly lashed lids lowered halfway as he bridged the gap between them.

Jasmine closed her eyes, desperately trying to control her trembling knees as she waited for the touch of his skin on her lips. His strong fingers slipped behind her neck and cradled the back of her head in a protective grasp. Just when she thought she couldn't stand it any longer, she felt the smooth, supple touch of his mouth … on her forehead.

Disbelief and confusion entered her system, replacing the nervous exhalation present just moments before. She pulled away from his touch and placed her hands on her hips with a frown.

"Excuse me? I was thinking maybe a little more than a pat on the head would be a proper show of gratitude." Jasmine tried to remain calm, but after everything she had been through, his emotional distance effected her more deeply than anything else she had experienced up until this point.

Had she not been so full of fire, she might have noticed the way his fingertips stroked the palm of her hand where he had so gently held her before the kiss.

"You make it difficult to protect your honor, my Lady," he growled with a primal undertone that made her aware of his lusty emotions in no uncertain terms.

"That's what I'm talking about," she exclaimed, pushing the envelope as far as she could to see if he reacted. "I'm not any kind of Lady, let alone yours, and you have no idea who I am. How can you treat me the way you do? You know nothing about me."

He regarded her with a silent look, and any sign of what he was experiencing was cloaked carefully behind the shield of his azure tinted eyes.

"You're my Lady when you're with me. And you're indeed a tempting woman, but I know in my heart you mean more to me than I could dare to dream. It is my hope that you can see this for yourself one day and I might be the one to show you."

Jasmine instantly regretted her behavior and wondered how she could have acted so petulant and spoiled in front of this incredible man. She was normally so strong, so sure of herself, but next to Hayden her heart fluttered and even shared its tremors with the rest of her body; it was just a situation with which she had no experience.

Time to go to school then, she thought inwardly, and resolved to learn everything she could about his world and her own feelings.

"I'm sorry," she lifted her face proudly and looked him straight in the eye.

He smiled at her with a small shake of his head.

"You truly are an astonishing woman." For the smallest amount of time, she thought he intended to reach for her again, to touch her once more before they fell into their accepted roles.

"We must reach Ravenswood well before dark," he said in a way that suggested he needed to convince himself they must move on. "We really don't want to be there after the sun goes down."

"Ravenswood?" she repeated, her thoughts turning back to the morning. "Is that the place where that soldier was from, the one who split the time stack?"

"Indeed it is. Before the war it was a beautiful place, so full of life and magic."

"This question probably goes without saying, but ... " Jasmine hesitated a second, looking for the right words. "What's it like now?"

He rewarded her query with a haunted look, and turned his eyes ahead as he spoke about the past.

"It's difficult to explain everything that has happened in our history, but as I told you before, the existence of our world was based on knowledge. We all felt God had given us the gift to learn from the mistakes of others and our religion was absolute. The holy order of Darkenbane studied the realms we crossed with a pledge to never intercede. It was our divine duty to follow the prophecy and the law."

“Right, sounds pretty ideal and all that, but something obviously happened,” Jasmine said as gently as she could without imposing an ‘I told you so’ tone.

“The Brotherhood of the Bane developed without any warning. They believed they could interfere, that they should change time as we all knew it. No one knows when it happened, it could be now, before or tomorrow ... ” He trailed off, his sadness obvious throughout the story.

“The Brotherhood of the Bane.” Jasmine chewed the words over in her mind. “So, you mean BOB is coming to get us?”

If he caught on to her wryly humorous tone, his face didn’t show it. His thoughts appeared to be turned inward and when he spoke again, his troubled eyes remained forward.

“The war started when I was a boy. To be perfectly honest with you, Jasmine—” He smiled to himself when he spoke her name. “The remaining pious monks of Darkenbane, and those of us who still fight for good, are nothing more than pockets of resistance throughout the greater kingdoms. The Brotherhood came for us a long time ago.”

“Well, can’t you just go back to before it all happened, and put a stop to it then?” Jasmine asked thoughtfully. “After all, it’s what your people do best, right?”

“If there was just one question asked most often about the war, you have spoken it. There are complications when traveling under the best of conditions, but the Brotherhood has weakened the timelines they travel to and the science we employed before has unpredictable results now.”

“That’s how you ended up with me.” She kept pace with him, realizing they had covered quite a lot of distance while she was so absorbed in the conversation. The large, rolling hills at the foot of the mountains had given way to a clear plain and traversing the terrain was becoming much easier.

“It’s true I didn’t expect to find a woman whose beauty was beyond compare, when I tracked this last path through the ring.” His tone was lighter and she wasn’t able to tell if he was teasing her. “It was unfortunate that I met up with a group of Bane Mercenaries as I cleared the entryway, but I could never curse my luck from the moment I saw your face.”

He looked at her as he spoke that last sentence, and though she could see how much better he was feeling, she still wasn't sure if his words were lighthearted for her benefit or part of his emotions.

"So, you can do the time thing too, then?" Jasmine asked, trying to get herself off the topic of his possible feelings. The direct attention of his serious blue eyes caused her breathing to become a bit irregular and she didn't want him to think she was too out of shape as the trail they followed began to wind through small copses of trees and shrubbery.

"All members of the royal family are taught from birth to practice timespace manipulation. The adept skill for it has long run through our bloodline," he answered her as if his lineage was not important.

Great, Jasmine thought to herself. *Let's just hope he's a third cousin of a Duke who vanquished a dragon fifty years ago and nothing more, or I'll never have a chance.*

"Wait. You said you tracked a path through the ring to my shop. Does that mean someone from the Brotherhood had been there?" She was instantly aware of the danger she could have been in.

"Someone had gone there, but I cannot tell if it was the hand of the Brotherhood or another. I travel every crossed path I encounter, in the hope I will fulfill my destiny and find the lost prophecies of my people."

"Well, if that's what we have to do, I'm going to need a change of underwear ... " She noticed the mountains were very far behind and a dark, menacing forest loomed ahead in the distance. To make matters worse, fog was even settling at the tree line ahead and curling up in offensive little wisps of doom.

'I'm not going in there." Jasmine planted both her feet and stared straight at the thick wall of trees as if it had gone out of its way to personally offend her.

"Ah." He sighed, seeing the misty barrier at the edge of the forest. "I had hoped to make it before dusk. It is possible that we can still break through before total darkness comes."

"It's also possible that I'm not going in there at night," she said testily. "I read *The Hobbit.* I know all about Mirkwood and I know there are probably giant spiders in there."

"There are no such things as giant spiders, Jasmine." His voice was reasonably amused. "What makes you think there would be any here?"

"Oh, I don't know," she said a bit sharply. "Maybe the Magic Kingdoms, or the Handsome Princes, or the Time Travelers ... and all the other things I didn't think were real before last night."

"While there are no spiders of unusual size, there are a lot of other dangers if you step off the path, and that's much easier to do in the darkness."

"That sounds familiar," she muttered under her breath, but she was glad he was willing to wait until the morning.

"I'm afraid we won't have the luxury of a haunted cabin tonight," he said to her with a grin and she knew now that there was a chance he might be developing a sense of humor. "We can stay near the border of the trees but not at the edge. The mist can pull you in, if you're not careful."

Jasmine thought of all the Stephen King stories she had read in her life, and didn't doubt it for a second.

◆

It was a tight, circular clearing within the tiny crop of trees, almost like it had been made for two people. The ground in the center was blanketed with fragrant pine needles, most still so green they were soft and inviting to lie on.

"We'll have to start a fire on our own in here, I'm afraid," Hayden said as soon as they found the spot. "I can't be certain the light from the flame won't be visible past our camp, but judging from the density of the fog this evening, we're going to have a drastic drop in temperature."

"Let's just hope we can find a way to stay warm," Jasmine added pointedly, walking around the edge to gather kindling. She had already done this at the cabin and if the Girl Scouts gave out patches to resourceful time travelers, she'd have one in her mailbox when she got home.

She had freshened up as much as she could with her travel kit back at the cabin, but she suspected she was a little worse for the wear in her torn T-shirt and muddy shoes. Hayden had some type of shoulder pouch made from the same brown leather as the rest of his outer clothing and it seemed to hold a million things, from a tinderbox to a canteen of water. She thought briefly of the secret cache in the fireplace that morning and wondered if there could be more space inside than out before she dismissed the idea as too many games of Dungeons and Dragons as a child.

Before she could even think about fishing the matches out of her comparatively large bag, he had a small blaze started near the edge of their cozy little hideaway. The clearing itself acted as a chimney, directing the smoke in an upward spiral.

When he saw the flame was steady and under control, he turned to her.

"There's a small stream nearby. I'm going to check the water and scout out the area at our back for signs of our firelight. You will be safe if you remain here until I return."

She glanced up at the dimming sky, and realized they must have traveled a great distance for night to have come so soon. With a reluctant nod, she watched him make his way through the closely gathered trees. Jasmine suddenly thought of all the things he might need if he was going to be out more than a few minutes. With the darkness coming in so quickly, she wondered if she was more worried about him going alone, or being left herself like a child who might get into trouble. After at least a whole minute had passed, she decided to follow his lead. After all, how far could he have gotten?

Hayden was definitely more skilled at traversing the heavily wooded ring, but she plodded on as carefully as she could, always seeing one twig ahead just springing back and leading her on. It seemed like she had been pushing her way through the branches forever, when she looked down and saw the scratches on her hands in the dim light.

Just as she was about to turn back, she heard the sound of a bubbling stream directly in front of her through the trees. It was almost completely dark now and she sighed with relief, thinking of the apology she would make to Hayden for straying from the plan. *He probably has a torch or lantern inside his bottomless pouch.*

The heavy foliage finally gave way to an open area, and she stepped foot onto a smooth bed of grass. The moon was full and the blades at her feet dripped with moisture as if they were painted in liquid silver.

She turned to look behind her and the leaves of the forest looked the same, nearly shining in the pale moonlight. There was no sign she had even passed through their barrier just a moment ago, and that made her very uncomfortable as she turned to follow the stream and find her handsome guide.

Hayden had said he went to scout behind them, which meant the direction they had come. Jasmine assumed if she followed the stream up, she'd cover that territory since the mountains would be its source.

All that was much easier said than done, however, as the embankment gradually became steep and treacherous the further she went. The stream stretched wider and was trying its best to be a river as the width expanded more and more with each additional step. She thought she should turn back, but had to admit to herself that if she didn't find her friend she was in trouble. She had no idea where she left the woods and hadn't marked the spot.

The water flow was rapid now as she walked and she noticed a swirl of currents on the surface. The edge she gingerly traversed was almost a cliff and she instantly saw the reason why just ahead. A beautiful waterfall cascaded from a series of naturally step-shaped rock formations and into the newly classified river below.

She stood, entranced, as the water poured from its source and into the pool far beneath her feet. It rippled out in hypnotic waves from the turbulent spawn point into a still basin of water before the tranquil haven gave in to the river that fed the current.

His back was to her, and she covered her mouth to suppress the gasp that instinctively escaped. He stood waist-deep in the languid part of the pool, his muscular back rippling as his hands cupped the sparkling water he poured over his skin. His exposed hips were perfect, taut and toned as he twisted slightly, revealing his lower back. Thick, blonde hair clung to his shoulders and Jasmine could barely breathe, let alone recognize the fact that swirling tendrils of mist were engulfing her feet and ankles as she stood frozen in place.

The damp, painful chill alerted her just moments later, but by then she was unable to move. The mist had circled up around her knees and approached her thighs when she truly began to panic.

"Hayden!" she cried out at the top of her lungs, straining to overcome the crash of the falls below. "Help me!"

The solitary figure stopped, and in slow motion, turned to face her. To her horror, she realized it was not Hayden at all, but a man in a mask. Grotesque horns twisted from the top, and an animal's face regarded her with interest.

Something deep and primal rose up inside her very soul, driven by fear and passion. The thought of the hunt and the price she would pay for being caught. She saw the creature in the pool in all his glory. Strong and proud he stood before her, unashamed of his state of arousal, and she ... an innocent waiting to be caught.

The mist ensconced her up to the waist now, and she shivered from the icy touch of its imprisoning fingers. A primitive part of her body wanted to be tamed by the life lessons that governed all those who exist, yet another part of her heart longed for the mysterious man back in the clearing and she silently cursed herself for venturing beyond her boundaries.

She tried to scream when the creature appeared in front of her, so close it seemed he was touching her. His eyes were beyond intelligent behind the mask, but it was his scent that made her dizzy. All at once he smelled like life, death and the musky fragrance of a thousand dreams of love and longing.

Her soul fought as the wispy web cocooned the last piece of physical resistance she had to offer the God of the Grove.

I knew there were faeries on the other side of the fountain, her last thought surfaced, as the ethereal threads caressed her lips and wove its freezing touch throughout her curls. For the first time in her life, Jasmine was totally helpless and at the whim of her captor.

Chapter Five

The voices were distant. She thought she might be underwater at first, but as she focused on the sounds, the distortion cleared and she was able to make out the words and a few degrees of light and darkness beyond her obscured vision.

"She is not from this world, and therefore, not subject to your laws," a low, frustrated voice spoke at the very edge of her hearing.

"She entered my domain willingly." The response was swift and terrible; it definitely stood for no argument, as if the rules were age-old and proven.

"I am still the royal heir to the throne," the one pleading her case said with clear threat in his voice. "While that does not count for much at the moment, if we should prevail ... "

"You do not have to tell me what it would mean if you prove victorious." The voice she came to recognize as that of her captor spoke calmly. "You have a skill that I have not. Perhaps we could make a bargain."

"It would be outside of the law for me to agree to such a treaty!" She knew then it was Hayden who continued to negotiate her freedom, and her heart lit at the sound of his voice.

"Hayden." She struggled with absolute concentration to force the sound past her frozen lips.

Silence instantly filled the room and she was conscious of the fact her words were the focal point.

"Impossible," her assailant breathed, and both shadows came closer to her location. "She cannot be lucid at this point. She must be more valuable than your case represented ... "

The sly tone in his words was not missed by Hayden, and he instantly stepped up.

"I will make the bargain you decree."

"So the royal bloodline does falter, just as the prophecy states … " The insidious implication dwindled off and she knew they had turned their backs to her. It was just as well, for she hadn't the strength for such a show again.

"What do you know of the prophecy?" Hayden's voice exploded in anger from the distance, and she was afraid he would forget his promise to free her for a moment, the intensity was so great.

"Surely I know nothing you do not," the antagonizing voice said with mock consolation. "Shall we begin our part of the bargain?"

"Let me prepare my confession." Hayden's words were strong and sure, leaving no doubt about his intentions. The exertion it took to break free from her bondage cost her dearly in the icy trap, and her consciousness faded into a cloud of grey with the footsteps that echoed away.

◆

It was difficult to breathe, but Jasmine tried not to panic. Her skin was freezing, and it felt like a thousand needles pricked her hands and feet. If she tried very hard she could move them a little bit, and at least she could hear and see again. The crackling pine in the fire sent off sparklers of color and sound, and that light helped her focus on the here and now. The rest of her limbs were numb and her lips were surely blue, but the hot breath that warmed her face with promises rallied the rest of her senses, and she was determined that she wasn't going to sleep through the attentions of her hero.

It wasn't quite what she expected, however.

"Damn this forest magic," he swore, his tone as fiery as his anger and she could even see the flame from the campfire flicker in his luminous orbs as if he were the very devil himself. "I asked you to do one thing, and I should have known well enough that you wouldn't."

But Jasmine could see past the façade of the firelight reflection to the lines of concern on his face. She would have been well on her way to joy that he felt so passionately for her, if the pricking needles were not beginning to work their way up her arms and legs. The sensation was unlike anything she had ever physically felt in her entire life, and if she hadn't been lying in Hayden's arms, she thought she couldn't possibly come close to surviving it.

Her teeth began to chatter in a most embarrassing manner, and no matter how hard she tried, she couldn't stop shivering.

Hayden pulled her close when her body started to lose control, and he held her tightly to his chest as if he could absorb her agony into his own body by sheer proximity alone.

"Please stay with me," he whispered, his cheek pressed against hers. "I cannot bear to lose you again, beautiful girl."

His fingers stroked her hair, and every place his skin made contact with her body the pain eased a slight amount.

Jasmine was sure she was dreaming for a moment. She was at the fountain and the water fell with a tranquil grace into the basin below. The sun struck the clouds away for one second and they shrank against the lovely rays of light. Beautiful, warm ribbons of golden streams fell onto her face and she saw him again for the first time when she turned. But he reached his youthful fingers out to touch her curls, not grasp her hand nervously as she thought she remembered well.

"This fountain holds my destiny," he said to her, and pulled her tightly to him. She braced herself for the thunder, the cries of terror ... but they never came. As the water bubbled on the edge of her awareness, she began to feel the pain subside though she had lost her total sense of identity. The only thing at the forefront of her mind at the moment was the fact that she was warm and safe. Her primal need to live overcame everything and she reached out for the man who was keeping her alive.

"You must fight for me, Jasmine." Hayden's voice cut through the haze and she knew he was the one who saved her from her icy fate. "The God of the Grove takes his women to the brink of death so the instinct of survival alone brings out their ultimate passion. You must be stronger than his spell to live past his devious plan for your honor."

His voice was urgent, strong, and that alone drove her to a distraction that could only be described as pure need. She was dying and she knew it. In her delirium, she thought the only way to save her life was to take him inside of her; only then could she bring both of them together into the world of the living by the very act of creation.

Her lips found his by instinct, as if they were drawn to them by an irresistible force.

Yes! Her thoughts exploded as his hot, wet kiss shocked the core of her existence. This was the way it was meant to be.

"Jasmine, please," he begged between the ardent play for his tongue. "You must not tempt me in this manner. Every fiber in my being longs to take you now, but if I do, I could never forgive myself for such an action against a woman helpless under the influence of another."

She heard his words like a distant memory, but it penetrated the spell she was under. Though she couldn't prevent her body from straining to touch him in every way possible, she knew with dismay that her actions could condemn his sense of honor. She didn't ever want to be the subject of his regret and she cried hot tears of remorse. They trailed down her cold cheeks and steamed in the firelight. As the warm liquid fell, her skin seemed to thaw and the urgent desire was replaced by her concern about what he must think of her.

"And there it is; your heart is stronger than any magic, and it will always save us both." He traced her trail of tears with a reverent fingertip, letting her own body feel her humanity.

It felt like a long dip in a hot bath. Slow at first on her toes, but it spread upward like waves lapping at her feet in a lazy tropical inlet. She lay against him as helpless as a baby as he continued to gently stroke her thawing skin with a tenderness she had never known in all her life.

She had no choice but to trust him next to the blaze of their fire. Her traumatized body registered the heat as a chilling assault, but she knew that it had to be warm.

"I am so sorry." She forced the words out through her clenched and chattering jaw. "Thank you for protecting me."

The firelight danced against her closed eyelids and as she struggled to define the difference between reality and illusion, she briefly thought of Plato's *Allegory of the Cave.* In that story, a whole generation of people had lived their entire lives facing a cave wall, only seeing the shadows of their world cast in front of them by unseen flames at their back. When asked which was real, the objects they had never seen or the shadows they cast, they chose the shadows, which was only thing they ever knew. For the first time in her life, that tale made sense to her, and although she thought she might be crazy, all she had before her was this reality to accept.

"I will always come for you," Hayden whispered, his soft lips touching her forehead, and her memories of the dream began to mingle with the perception of what was happening at present.

All of this is funny, Jasmine thought ironically. The dream had held court in the realm of her imagination for as long as she could remember, but always as make-believe. Now she slipped into a world that felt more like home to her than the place where she grew up and almost instantly she had accepted it. She briefly wondered if that is what crazy people do—if one day they wake up and find a hole in the universe down in their basement or something, only no one will believe them even they know they're the only ones who can stop whatever evil plot is set up to destroy the world.

She was a bit concerned she really didn't find any of the things that were happening overly surreal, but that worry soon subsided as comfortable darkness and exhaustion took over. Whatever happened after this was beyond her control now, but that was nothing unusual. And somehow she knew the dream wasn't coming.

◆

Jasmine took a brief look at her damp, muddy jeans and torn T-shirt. It occurred to her she was probably not the most ravishing creature on the other side of the fountain right now, but she was still acutely conscious of the fact that Hayden had held her tenderly all night, keeping watch without so much as a kiss or improper move. In fact, he was still curled up on the soft pine needles and probably experiencing actual sleep for the first time since the sun crested the sky and lit the circle over head.

She made herself busy with the fire, and since the coals still lingered with a warm glow in the ashes, it sprang to life with an impressive show that hinted at a lot more work than she had done.

Quite proud of herself at the accomplishment, she sat on the edge of the clearing and watched him sleep the dawn away. Relaxing a bit for the first time since all this began, she remembered the old leather book in her bag and carefully drew it out to inspect it in the daylight. Much to her disappointment, the thick pages had absorbed nearly all of the ink, and smudges were just about all that was visible. Still, she touched the exquisite paper with her fingertips, a longing look in her eyes for the past and what might have been written there.

Hayden watched her for quite a while as she turned the pages, but didn't think to alert her to his wakeful state. His eyes were warm and passionate as he took in her serene movements, but as she turned to glance his way he hid his emotion admirably.

"What were you reading?" he asked her softly, because he could tell that the object had some kind of profound effect on her.

"It's just an old book, left to me by someone in the family." She shrugged off its importance to her, mostly because she couldn't explain why it meant so much.

He looked at her as if he knew she wasn't being totally truthful, so she tossed it to him casually. Her heart skipped a beat for a moment as it arced through the air, but with the grace of a feline Hayden reached up and caught it easily.

"Interesting," he said to himself, looking at the leather binding before he opened it to the first page. His brow furrowed as he quickly learned that the pages were illegible at best, and blank at the worst.

"I hope to copy the words inside, and preserve some of my family history," Jasmine spoke tentatively, with a look of hope on her face that he didn't dare to tease.

His smile was genuine as he rose to his feet, and crossed the distance to lay the book in her hands. For a moment his touch lingered on her skin. She was instantly overwhelmed by the way it made her feel and surprised that every contact she had with him never lessened it.

"I know you will tell your tale with strength and spirit. Your people will be proud for generations to come." His warm, blue eyes assured her and she wanted nothing more at that moment than to fling herself into his arms, but she couldn't read any signals from him that might tell her it would be okay.

"Well," she changed the subject as she lowered her eyes and rummaged through her bag, "I have some peanuts from the flight to start with. They are honey coated, but I still think they might be edible. The flight crew was generous that day and I got two bags, so we won't starve."

"Now that we have daylight, our travel time to the monastery will be minimal," he assured her, but she wasn't sure she was all too happy about that. "When we arrive, there will be warm greetings and a feast for the one who saved my life."

"And that is in the woods?" She wanted to know how far they had to go, but after her experience the last evening, she was a little reticent to go anywhere near the forest

He looked at her openly, and she saw strength and understanding in his eyes.

"As long as you remain by my side, nothing will come between us."

His honest and simple tone lent her courage and as he offered his hand she walked across the clearing to join him.

"It's so hard for me to believe you're real," she sighed as she surrendered her fingers to his touch.

"My Lady Jasmine," he addressed her softly as he brought the back of her hand to his face and laid it against his cheek. "It is so hard for me not to show you how real I am."

He didn't stop her from turning her palm to his cheek, but he closed his eyes and drew in a deep breath when she did so. His hand still cradled her touch, and pressed her more firmly against his skin as if he couldn't bear to let her go.

"I thought I was the best man I could be." He opened his eyes and looked at her with clear desire on his face. "I had my destiny and my kingdom and I never faltered on my journey. But when I look at you, I suspect there is so much more that I could become." With a gentle motion, he set her hand by her side and took a step back as if waiting for something.

"How about those peanuts?" he said somberly, and she realized her stomach was rumbling a bit loudly. She was instantly embarrassed and all of a sudden a feast at the monastery didn't sound that bad in the least.

Packing up the camp consisted of covering the fire and making sure it was out. Jasmine ducked behind a tree with the excuse of using the bathroom, but after making quick work of it, pulled out her travel bag and toothpaste.

I may be in some medieval realm, she thought to herself, *but I'm going to brush my teeth and put on some lipstick!*

She made sure she didn't go out of the line of sight for the camp, but when she came back to the clearing and found herself alone, she was a little nervous. The feeling didn't last long, however, when her companion emerged a minute later. She noticed his teeth were sparkling white, too, and he had a shy smile on his face.

The smoldering ashes were dwindling into a safe state as they made their way out of the circle of trees. She wanted to ask him about the night before, about the God of the Grove, but a part of her wasn't sure if it might have been just another dream. Everything seemed so normal today, and he didn't give off a hint of the Savior cologne she sprinkled him with last evening.

It didn't take long for yesterday's thoughts to be dispelled as she came face to face with the wall of briars that made up the edge of the wood.

"I can't wait to see how you get us through this," Jasmine said, and stood back with her arms crossed.

"Do you trust me?" Hayden turned to her with a look on his face that left her no choice. She was surprised to find she really did.

"Sure, why not. Like I said before, you're the only person I know on the other side of the fountain. How does that work, anyway?" she asked.

"You know the ring you found, at the stone pile near the cabin?" He held up his left hand and in an exaggerated motion, swept the ring off his finger and stuck it against a huge tree at the very edge of the forest.

She half expected it to fall to the ground, but wasn't shocked when it didn't. Slowly, with his eyes still on hers, he drew his canteen of water and tipped the end into the ring. Immediately, a liquid surface formed, similar to what she might have seen in a bubble wand as a child. With a gentle touch, he simply reached out one finger and ran it around the perimeter of the silver loop. It expanded to the size of a large oval, and her jaw dropped in spite of herself.

The surface glimmered like a mirror reflecting waves, and she knew this was where her dream met reality. If she was going to ever believe it, she had to make a decision now, and she had to make the best one she could.

Hayden watched her carefully, and when he saw she was fully aware of the device and what was going to happen, he took her hand gently and pulled her toward the surface.

"I don't think so!" she exclaimed, holding back and planting her feet in the ground.

"Look inside the passage," he said softly, no sign of impatience in his voice.

Jasmine was compelled to gaze within the ripple and she saw a welcoming, if distorted, green path through the silver loop.

"How do I know it's real?" she asked, her doubtful eyes turning to his with the question. "On second thought, how can I know if anything is real at this point?"

"You have only my word," he said softly, but the tone of his voice let her know that his word was golden. "Remember that you have done this once already, though in the confusion you really had no choice. To earn your trust, I will enter first. I pray that you will follow my lead and join me, because the passage will close just minutes after initial contact."

With that said, he released her hand and touched the window. Like a blur from a wicked faery tale, he was gone. Jasmine took a second to consider the hostile trees before her, and the mist waiting in the wings to take her once again.

"Alright, I guess its sink or swim," she mumbled to herself, and took a long breath like she was about to dive into the deep end of the pool.

With brave and steady fingers, she reached out and touched the reflective surface of the ring. For one brief instant she felt pulled outside of her skin. Her thoughts and heart and soul seemed to rush ahead of her for just a few moments, before she poured into her body like a funnel emptying into a bowl on the other side.

Hayden caught her before she stumbled to the ground, and she was instantly thankful for that.

"It is most difficult the first few passages and you have been through twice now," he assured her in what was probably a comforting tone, though words didn't hold a lot of solace at the moment. "It will get better."

"How many more times do I have to do this?" She turned to face him, her stomach pitching like it was in two different places at once.

"Oh, I don't know," he answered nonchalantly. ""How many changes of underwear do you have?"

"If you think I'm not in, you're wrong," she gritted between her teeth, catching her breath and standing as straight as she could before him.

"You impress me more and more." He held her by the arms. "If I didn't know any better, I'd think you had a noble blood line and possessed the talent as well."

"I don't know how noble I am," she started, coming to grips with the displaced feeling that was already leaving her system, "but I do know I am a royal pain in the ... "

She spun about as the thundering echo of hoof beats assaulted the pair in the glade. Before she could utter a cry in protest, they found themselves surrounded by a regiment of horsemen, fully decked out in shining silver plate.

With a strong and subtle movement, Hayden pushed her behind him. For once in her life, Jasmine didn't complain about the chivalry.

The lead horse was almost prancing, its rider in a purple plumed helm, expertly sitting upon the magnificent mount.

As they pair approached, Jasmine felt her protector relax and walk away from her to meet the mounted challenger.

She extended a hand to his retreating back as he left her behind, but lowered it when the rider dismounted with a cry of pleasure. He swept off his helm to reveal a chestnut brown beard and handsome dark eyes.

"My Lord, you have returned." He kneeled before her companion, and Jasmine felt a shiver up her spine at his reverence.

"It is good to see you once more, Malcolm," Hayden spoke with deep joy, and Jasmine froze as he turned his eyes to hers. He nodded briefly, to acknowledge her recognition and to plead with her not to give it all away.

"Jasmine." Hayden turned formally to her. "My I present my Captain of the Guard, Malcolm of Ravenswood."

"It is an honor, My Lord." She curtsied in a self conscience manner, well aware her knowledge of antiquated etiquette may not be the standard here.

"A true beauty you bring among us, Sire!" The captain clapped Hayden on the back, but gave Jasmine a respectful look.

"Have you come to escort us to the monastery?" he inquired in a harmless enough manner, looking for all the world like the task was nothing and they hadn't read the confession at the cabin just that morning.

"And I always have, My Lord Amarynn." Malcolm laughed as if

he thought he was jesting.

Jasmine gave Hayden a sharp look at the way the captain addressed him, but he shrugged as if it were a common thing and motioned for her to join them on horseback. Living in California most of her life, she had a lot of experience with horses and at this point in time could think of nothing she was more grateful for. A dark mare was brought to her, with a black and golden leather saddle.

"Pretty girl," she whispered in her horse's ear, before she mounted the obedient steed. "What's her name?"

"Nightwish," a nearby soldier answered her with pride, and Jasmine reached down to stroke her face with tenderness.

"Stay close by my side," Hayden instructed abruptly, cutting through her reverie. As if on command, Nightwish rode forward and stood beside the stallion they had given to her companion.

"Where are we?" she whispered, looking carefully around to see if anyone noticed her stealthy attempt at conversation. "Strike that. *When* are we?"

"We're only inside one dissection of the timeline, Jasmine," Hayden whispered to her as they rode next to each other. "We have yet to arrive at the gateway to the Monastery. I had no way of knowing what would be waiting for us during this pass, the lines so often blur and overlap in Ravenswood."

"Do you mean we have to go through another ring?" she hissed under her breath, trying to stay as close to him as she could.

"How do you think a time war is fought, beautiful girl?" he regarded her with steely eyes. "The entire wood is shattered into countless slivers of reality. This is where the fight began, after all."

"So you're saying it's possible that Malcolm's family might not be dead yet?" She said it with such a high-pitched urgency that he swiftly looked around to see they drew attention.

"I have no way of knowing when they died," he answered her quietly. "To Malcolm, a short few days may have passed since we met last, but for me it could have months. All time instances here are random."

"Then you have to say something," she insisted, and his jaw line clenched with helpless frustration.

"We're not permitted to interfere with history. If we choose to take time into our own hands, we would be no better than the

Brotherhood and corruption would surely follow."

"That's a chance you have to take, really." She held his gaze for a moment and he saw her conviction. Just as he broke eye contact with a shake of his head, the party slowed to a stop.

"We have arrived, My Lord." Malcolm slid easily off his horse and offered his hand to Jasmine with a smile on his face. Instead of answering his kindness with a word, she slipped from her mount with a plea in her eyes for Hayden.

It was only a moment before she saw the glimmering ring just ahead, and she stepped before it with resignation.

"So, I guess you really are Lord Amarynn," she said with no small amount of surprise, but a little sadness.

"I am." He turned to her with such strength and pride that her respect for him caused her heart to beat with a thrill.

"And you don't have any uncles that have slain dragons?" She raised her eyebrow with a little hope.

"I am afraid not, My Lady." He bowed before her so properly that she felt as if she were the queen of a long forgotten realm.

"Then do one thing for me," she stated flatly, glancing at Malcolm as she turned to the circle. With no visible signs of reluctance, she touched the surface and was gone in an instant.

"I already have," he spoke solemnly to the empty spot where she had been standing and expelled a deep sigh.

"Malcolm," Hayden said to his captain, motioning for him to approach. "There is one more task you must perform for me."

"Immediately," his loyal servant answered without question. "Just tell me what it is."

♦

It was so dark under the thick canopy of leaves that she couldn't be sure what time of day it was. Not that any amount of sunshine could penetrate the heavy cover above her head, but just knowing there was daylight out there somewhere made her feel better.

As her eyes adjusted to the gloom, Jasmine anxiously watched the place where she first appeared for a sign Hayden was right behind her. He told her if they stayed together, nothing could happen to her, and she was beginning to wonder if she might have given those words of wisdom a little more consideration before she so easily went ahead on her own.

After a few short minutes passed as an eternity in her mind, she started pacing back and forth. There was an obvious path leading away from her location in one direction, so at least if she had to make a choice, there was only one way to go.

The increasing frequency of rustling leaves and snapping twigs might have been her imagination, but she was getting spooked all the same. Just when she convinced herself that it was nothing to worry about, a low and feral grow came from the bushes at her back. She spun around in time to catch a glimpse of yellow, glowing eyes and all of a sudden the last place she wanted to be was inside another forest in the dark.

Very slowly, she backed up to the spot where she thought the path was. With a strong and determined chin, she carefully walked away from the clearing as if she had nothing in the world to fear. She almost laughed as she broke free of the oppressive forest in less than fifty yards.

"I knew it was night!" The moon was waning full and it shone down on the rolling hills at her feet. She followed the valley with her eyes, and saw in the distance what had to be the monastery.

It was a glorious, ancient and gothic structure; everything she thought a secret, monk filled conservatory should be. Warm lights flooded through the windows, and the cold night at her back urged her toward the obvious source of safety and comfort.

What are you doing? She panted to herself as she plodded through the valley and across the perfect lawn to the huge, wooden doors of the structure.

Deciding she wasn't going to punish herself for going ahead of Hayden when he so obviously left her to linger alone, Jasmine reached out and grasped one of the twin iron door knockers which adorned the time darkened planks. It must have weighed twenty pounds, because it was quite a struggle to get it up.

The blow from the knocker to the wood could have given her a concussion, the resulting boom was so deep and resonant, but she recovered from the shocking jar and wondered if there was a doorbell somewhere instead.

The rusted iron that braced the scarred doors wept for her a trail of rejection, and she was about to turn away when a crack appeared in the weathered, onyx studded barrier.

"Name, please," the mouse-like voice squeaked through the opening in a suspicious manner, like she was an uninvited guest who showed up at a dinner party selling Amway.

"Jasmine," she answered honestly, not knowing anything else to say.

"No, no Jasmine is not on the list, I'm afraid." He sounded very apologetic in a tired, rehearsed way. "Who are you a guest of?"

She thought for a moment of all the names she had heard on this adventure. "My Lord Amarynn?" The words came out like a question, and she was just unsure enough that he didn't buy it.

"My Lady," he told her gently with a chuckle. "If you were the guest of Lord Amarynn, we'd have the red carpet rolled out for you. In case you haven't noticed, you're at the back door."

"This is the back door?" She looked at the hinges alone that were bigger than the size of her head.

"And if she were the guest of Lord Amarynn?" A strong, passionate voice came from behind her, resounding with disappointment.

There was no immediate answer, because all the guards behind the door were suddenly outside and kneeling on the obviously absent red carpet.

Jasmine felt like the Queen of England ... better than the Queen! Hayden took her hand and guided her past the prostrate servants who had barred her entry just moments before.

Her ragged jeans could have been made of flowing silver. Her frazzled tresses might have been dressed with ribbons so fine. Her unpainted face glowed like—

"You have brought before us a lost and weary traveler," a highly cultured voice spoke with all the warmth and compassion of a glacier heading south for the winter.

"I greet you, Lady Cordelia," her escort spoke with civility to the strange woman who had appeared before them so magically in the servant's hall.

"May I introduce My Lady Jasmine," Hayden spoke smoothly, but she noticed a strained sense of concern in his tone.

The woman moved toward them with a glowing essence of vitality. To Jasmine, she was extraordinarily beautiful with light, flaxen colored hair and eyes of cold, grey steel. Her skin was so regal and pale that it was practically translucent, though she had a disdainful air about her as she raked her chilly, clear eyes over Jasmine's figure.

She looked down at her torn shirt and dirty clothes. It took only a moment for Jasmine to realize that her presence was not acceptable. For the first time since all of this began, she actually wished this was a dream.

She self consciously wiped her stained hands against her denim clad hip, and made a move closer to Hayden, but Cordelia was quick to grab her arm before she reached him.

"Let me take you to prepare, my friend." She smiled like a snake before her. "For no guest of Lord Amarynn could be his shame at a dinner in his honor … "

Jasmine looked over her shoulder as she was pulled away, and saw Hayden surrounded by friends and family that were obviously happy to see him safe. She only hoped she hadn't caused him any more embarrassment than necessary and allowed herself to be lead by the firm grip of the lady next to her.

She was already well down the corridor before Hayden turned with searching eyes through the crowd, and they burned with passion when he couldn't seek her out. The look on his face was lost to Jasmine, but not to the frowning woman at her side.

"After all," Cordelia said a bit stiffly, in a wicked way that left her feeling terrible inside, "what would they say about Lady Amarynn if she didn't graciously show hospitality to every wandering waif his Lordship dragged in?"

She may as well have slapped Jasmine in the face with her words, and the smug look of triumph Cordelia wore hung like an ugly mask over her beauty. She swept out of the room as quickly as she had come in, leaving nothing behind but stunned silence.

Chapter Six

The first few times she heard the knock at the door it was polite and full of restraint. Unfortunately, the longer she chose not to respond to the inquiry brought additional rounds of more urgent pounding through the heavily barred oak. She was forced to put her head under the pillow to diffuse the annoying sound.

The four-post bed that she was currently occupying was well dressed in lush silken wraps, with embroidered beads along the edges of the pillow shams, but Jasmine didn't really care about that. In fact, she wiped the tears from her face on the exotic looking cover and thought about everything that had happened the past few days.

It was funny ... Most of her life she had rarely cried over anything—not that she was an orphan, not that she fell through a fountain and ended up in a strange world that was probably not real. It started when Hayden read Malcolm's letter at the cabin, and her feelings had been running rampant ever since. The simple fact she thought she was in love with some guy from another dimension didn't rattle her half as much as the knowledge he had a wife. How could he have been so tender with her these past few days, when all along Ms. Iceberg 2008 was at home waiting in the wings to crash her ship of dreams?

After careful consideration, she realized he had been very adamant about her honor throughout the entire adventure, and now she knew why. Her heart ached in her chest and she really thought she was going to die from it.

Maybe if I put enough pillows over my head this will go away and I'll wake up somewhere in a hospital asking for more pain medication, she thought to herself, but nothing would make it better.

All the pillows in the world couldn't cover up the sound of her breaking heart ... or the tapping on her window, for that matter.

"What the ...?" She sat up in an explosion of cushions and fabric, grabbing the nearest one like a shield.

Hayden's face was clearly hovering in front of the glass, and his breath steamed up the outside of the pane. His complete look of distress encouraged her to rise and enjoy a better view. He was precariously hanging from some type of vine that didn't seem to give him a lot of confidence with regard to its support.

"Let me in," she heard him say a little desperately through the glass, and she took a moment to consider his words. She finally decided he had saved her from the God of the Grove no matter what his marital status was, so she should probably do him a solid favor in return.

"What in the all the realms are you doing in here?" he gasped as he struggled through the opening she had allowed. "Is everything alright?"

"Everything was fine before you sicked your wife on me," Jasmine responded sullenly, and returned to the bed to begin the process of burying herself in pillows once again.

"My wife?" He looked at her for the entire world like she was crazy. Jasmine didn't miss it, and allowed her head to surface above the folds.

"Yeah, the Wicked Witch of the West, Cordelia," she said, wishing she had a house or something handy to drop on the woman.

"Cordelia is not a witch." Hayden grinned. "Though sometimes I wonder about that. She is also not my wife, however much she may wish it to be."

This last statement interested Jasmine immensely and she looked at him suspiciously from behind the pile.

"But she said she was your wife."

"Think carefully, my Lady," he held her gaze steadily. "Did she ever actually say those direct words, or did she use a clever insinuation?"

"Now that you mention it, she was pretty slick about the whole thing." She thought back to the few words exchanged between them and she realized Cordelia had manipulated her. "Oh my God, I am so dense sometimes." Jasmine planted her face in her hands.

"More likely that you have a beautiful heart, incapable of such duplicity and so you couldn't conceive of it."

Jasmine removed her hands and watched him as he stood in the center of the room. For the first time since she had arrived, she noticed the nice furnishings and tapestries all around the stone chamber.

"Cordelia's family and mine were once both in line to rule and we could have been betrothed at a young age, that is true," he explained, as he began to pace across the rug in front of the fire. "But the monarchy suffered a fatal blow by the Brotherhood of the Bane, and such foolish notions were stricken from our traditional operations."

"Something tells me she's not okay with that," Jasmine spoke wryly, and climbed from the high mattress set where she had been perched. "Anyway, you said this was a monastery." She gestured widely around at the obvious sumptuousness of the room. "Looks more like a castle filled with lords and ladies, if you ask me. Not that you did ... "

"This is the last safe place against the Brotherhood." He couldn't help but smile at her observation. "The Holy Order of Darkenbane opened its doors when there was no place left to go."

"How kind of them," Jasmine said sourly. "Did they have to let Cordelia in?"

"It is a kindness, for sure. But not that unusual, considering half the members of the order are royal family members in one way or another."

Silence followed his statement, and she felt a little awkward all of a sudden, like she had forgotten her lines in a play.

"If you don't have any other questions, I will get to the reason while I scaled my own castle wall to gain an audience with you." He took two long strides and came very close to her, next to the bed. "I would like to inquire after your escort for this evening's dinner party, my Lady. And if you have none, may I offer you my arm?"

"That's all pretty proper." Jasmine actually blushed as a result of his shift in mood and demeanor. "After all, we had peanuts together this morning and everything."

He bowed slightly, low enough that he could look up into her eyes. Her knees trembled a little bit at all the ceremony. She could see he was not joking, and assumed a straight face herself.

"Though my suitors were breaking down the door just one moment ago, you're the first to reach me and so I will accept your offer."

"As you wish, my Lady." He nodded to her formally. "I shall have Griff record your answer in the annals."

"You mean someone has to write down if we went to dinner or not?" she asked incredulously, more aware than ever that she was a stranger in this place.

"In some cases, it must be done," he said, and she got the feeling he was making it out to be less of a deal than it was.

"I'm sure I'll impress everyone at the table tonight." She looked down at her well traveled clothing and made a face before adding, "I probably smell really good, too."

"You look beautiful to me." He smiled, and she didn't argue because he was obviously insane and you can't persuade a crazy person.

His gaze lingered on her face and she thought he was going to say something else before she was suddenly aware of just how close he was standing. She wished, more than anything in the world, that she was dressed in a much more tempting manner and it must have shown in her eyes.

"I'll speak with Cordelia and have her send you one of her girls to help you prepare for the evening." He grinned mischievously, walking over to the door. "Is it okay if I unbar this now?"

Jasmine wasn't really sure if she felt safe in the monastery with a witch running loose, but thought she should at least let the serving girl in because she didn't want to wear her jeans to dinner.

"Go ahead, but if you find me with a dagger in my back, Grissom and his CSI team are a long way off." She smirked, though his face was already set.

"No one will harm you under my care," he said firmly, and easily lifted the bar before he disappeared down the corridor.

Jasmine shivered, alone in the room. The fire was dying out, and she walked over to kneel on the plush carpet in front of the fireplace. She picked up a few perfectly sized pieces of wood and gently laid them on the flame.

A quick look around showed many items in the chamber were uniquely exquisite and probably made by hand, like her book. Maybe everything Hayden said to her was true and they took the best of what they saw throughout their travels and kept it for their own. How many artisans from her world were pushed aside by inexpensive labor and easy machines to make their products?

Either way, she loved it here. Despite the fact she currently huddled before a fire in dirty, unacceptable clothing, she felt like she belonged. There was no way to explain it, no knowledge that she could glean as to why her feelings had changed—and she had only experienced the dream one time since she'd arrived. That alone was wonderful enough to make her want to stay.

The tap at the door was very fearful and quiet. In fact, it was so light that Jasmine nearly missed it as she sat basking in the warm glow of the orange flame before her.

Though no additional sound presented itself, she thought she had better get up and have a look in the corridor.

She carefully edged the heavy door open a few inches as she cautiously looked into the hall beyond. The flames in the fireplace danced violently as the cold air from the stone passage swept through her crack. After a minute or two, she thought she heard breathing to the right of the frame and after bracing herself, threw the door open to confront whatever lay beyond.

The girl was young, and pressed so closely against the rough stone wall next to her door that Jasmine thought she might go flat in an effort to disappear from view. All she could see from her standpoint was very straight blonde hair pulled back in a severe ponytail. She was dressed in some kind of pinafore or something, but it was filthy and torn.

"Um, hey." Jasmine pulled together all of her compassion and kindness for the occasion. "That wall is pretty solid. I checked already."

The girl pulled her face away from the rock and looked at her with big, blue eyes.

"Are you the witch?" she asked with a tremor in her voice, and Jasmine burst out laughing the second the words came out. In fact, she laughed for so long that the urchin in the hall stepped back and regarded her with curiosity on her face.

"Did Cordelia tell you I was a witch?" She struggled through her words to breathe. "I was just saying the same thing about her," Jasmine exclaimed, a little put out that the other woman had taken her idea.

The girl in the corridor was obviously a child, but she had an intelligent look in her eyes and Jasmine took an instant liking to her.

"Come in before you catch a cold in that drafty hall." She opened the door wide, and though the girl hesitated a moment, she looked into Jasmine's eyes like a grown person might and nodded in a very adult manner. With no further questions, she walked inside. As she crossed the room, a distinctly ripe smell wafted past and Jasmine's eyes watered.

"My Lady has informed me that I shall prepare you for the evening," she said in a nervous voice, as if it was a line she had rehearsed many times on her way up to the chamber.

"I'm not the only one who needs 'preparing,'" Jasmine answered her, making a strong effort not to turn away from the stench that radiated off the child. "What is your name?"

"My mother called me Jesi," she said shyly now, her eyes cast down to the flagstones at her feet.

"Called you Jesi?" She watched the unfortunate girls face, expecting tears. To her surprise, the blonde haired waif lifted her chin and spoke proudly.

"I do not remember much about my family. I am told my mother, father and sister all died from the shift sickness. But I have survived to serve the good name of Lord Amarynn with pride."

A slow smile spread across Jasmine's face and she reached out to touch Jesi's shoulder.

"We're going to be friends, you and me," she said with no doubt. The brilliant look in the girl's eyes changed immediately to pain the moment she touched her. Instantly, she pushed Jasmine's hand away and turned with shame.

The child's pinafore shifted slightly and she saw the horrendous purple and black bruise on her young shoulder.

"What happened to you!" she exclaimed before she could stop herself and consider a more tactful line of questioning.

"I have rightly been punished by the Lady Cordelia's hand," Jesi answered her automatically, as if the response had been issued many times.

"Rightly my Aunt Fanny," Jasmine growled, and kneeled before the girl who had yet to look her in the eye again. "Tell me what really happened."

"The Lady Cordelia was kind enough to take me in after the death of my mother," the child began, but Jasmine still thought the words were contrived. "One day as I was choosing her gowns, she caught me holding a beautiful dress against my own figure in the mirror. She beat me as I deserved, and sent me to the stables to work out my term."

"That explains the smell, anyway," Jasmine murmured under her breath, then sunk to her knees as she wrapped her arms around the little girl. "I'm happy she sent you to me. I gladly accept you and no harm will come to you again as long as I have breath in my body."

Her last words came out as a strong and protective oath and for the first time since she met her, the girl had a look of hope in your eyes.

"So, does that mean we have a bathroom here?" she added, and thought she sure spent a lot of time wishing for such a thing that she always took for granted back home.

"Cordelia could send a slave to my Lady's bedchambers," Jesi said with a reproachful look in her eyes. "But she couldn't skimp on the bedchamber itself or Lord Amarynn would notice!"

"That's a yes, I take it," Jasmine breathed thankfully, and stood as she closed the outer door. Jesi took her hand and led her through an alcove that was fairly hidden by well placed tapestries in the design of the place.

It was strange looking for sure. There was a sunken bubble of marble nestled among a great array of shelves and ledges all along the far wall of the small room.

Jesi passed her hand over a bronzed plaque on the wall and immediately dim light radiated from every point. With another gesture that seemed magical, the water began to flow and fill up the pod, cascading over the rock shelves.

"Just so you know," Jasmine said in the strictest voice she could muster. "I am not the only person having a bath tonight, so in you go."

"Oh, thank you," Jesi breathed as if she had granted her a most fond desire.

The girl emerged completely clean, wrapped in what looked like a lush towel or blanket. Jasmine couldn't be sure, but whatever it was, it was a luxury that she never gave herself back home. She wondered briefly why such a simple thing was overlooked in the everyday life by the people of her realm. A hot, warm blanket after a bath was easily done, after all.

The girl's wet hair shone a beautiful, dark blonde in the firelight and Jasmine had to admit that she was eager for her turn in the wishing well.

"I will be back, my Lady," Jesi assured her with all earnest, and the child seemed so happy that she didn't doubt her word at all.

The water flowed over the stones and ledges. Mist floated just an inch or two above the pod as she slid inside. She thought if this wasn't heaven, then nothing was.

The water burned at first on her skin, and as she raised her arms from the pool, steam coalesced from her body. This was like every tropical island advertisement she had ever seen, plus some. Minutes seemed to stretch on and as her skin began to shrivel, she realized that she had a date that evening so she couldn't stay there forever.

Reluctantly she stood in the dim light, water pouring off her skin in waves. Rows of heated towels lined the edges of the bathroom easily within reach and she gladly took one.

Wrapped up in the generous, absorbent fabric, she left the alcove of tranquility and stepped into the main part of her chamber one more.

Everything was different! Jesi had made up the bed, the fire practically blazed in the hearth and an armament of clothing was laid out for Jasmine to see. The girl herself was dressed in clean and fine dark linen that set off her newly sparkling light hair. This child was a true beauty, and Jasmine found herself to be quite proud of that fact that she had helped her.

"My Lady Cordelia bade me to clean you but gave no instruction as to your wear. They let me keep my family's things and I hope that the clothing I have brought from my mother's old wardrobe pleases you. Will allow me to continue with the garments I chose?" The girl bowed low before her, but Jasmine felt ashamed she would prostrate herself like that in front of her and it made her uncomfortable.

"Stand up." Her tone was a little sharp, and Jesi stepped back in alarm. "These are the things that belonged to your family. By all means, wear what you want. Sheesh ... "

Her attention was captured by the beautiful silk dressing gowns that draped across the obliging furniture throughout the room. She had turned away from the girl next to her but if she had glanced over, the look of gratitude on the face of the child would have told her that the reasonable kindness earned any loyalty that might have been in question.

"Are all these for me?" Jasmine asked, drawn immediately to an emerald green gown that sparkled in the ambient light of the chamber.

"I thought it would match your eyes," Jesi breathed, and she excitedly grabbed up the fabric in an ethereal swirl that floated through the air like a cloud.

"Cordelia will be unhappy with your presence if you choose to wear this gown tonight." Her new dressing girl spoke demurely, eyes downcast.

"What is my status here, right now?" Jasmine turned to her with a nervous tone. "How much of what I say and do matter here at this place?"

"You're a guest of my Lord Amarynn, and your simple wishes should be indulged," she immediately repeated the words she had been taught before adding, "There are a dozen Ladies of the court already whispering about what you might wear and your manners."

"That's disturbing news," Jasmine sighed, thinking of all the unwanted attention that would come her way. She had never been much of a gossip or cared for social cliques in the least. "Then I expect we had better choose the green gown."

"Let me help you get ready," Jesi replied, her voice filled with relief that Jasmine accepted the dress though it was far out of fashion.

•

Their footsteps fell gracefully on the flagstone of the corridor as Jesi held the electric light high to guide their way through the patches of darkness. That was the first thing that caught her eye as they left her rooms; it looked like an old fashioned torch, but the end of the staff issued a soft glow of energy that didn't give off any heat. She remembered that Hayden told her his world might seem archaic at first, but that they had technology that may surpass things she had known.

Jasmine personally felt like she was equipped with an anti-gravity device that allowed her skirts to float above the floor as they made their way to the ball room and she constantly poked and prodded at it to see what her gown would do next.

"It is only a hoop, my Lady," Jesi said reproachfully, giving her a strange look in the torchlight and Jasmine left off the experiments for the time being.

The doors at the end of the hall were gilded and elaborate. Faeries and satyrs danced among the bronze sculpted artwork along the edges, just waiting to be touched by arriving guests.

There was no knocker on her side of the door, so she reached forward and obliged the frolicking woodland nymphs with a nudge. On silent hinges the heavy doors swung inward and every last remnant of reality that she might have been holding deep inside her mind was ripped away by what she saw inside.

Chapter Seven

As her eyes adjusted to the dim surroundings a deep, lush pulse began to throb through her veins and she understood that some type of music was playing in the distance. Although she felt she had control over her body, the sounds that echoed inside her head suggested that she step inside and experience the auditory pleasure more directly. When she entered the darkened room her movements slowed, but her vision began to clear.

A moment of panic gripped her when she realized she was standing inside an underwater landscape of mythic proportion. She had been unconsciously holding her breath, but gasped in surprise as a brightly colored fish swam past her nose. With great relief, she found she was able to draw air into her lungs.

"He said dinner, not swimming," Jasmine whispered to herself, but the entrancing vision of the deep blue waves pulled her further and further inside.

It almost felt like she was floating on the current when Hayden came out of nowhere and took her arm.

"It is only a Hologram," he spoke directly into her ear, though his words seemed taken along by the flow. "Bear with me this illusion; the court has too much time on their hands and not enough space since the war. The greatest honor they compete for these days is most impressive entrance to the dinner hall."

Trusting his word, she held onto his proffered arm like in the deal and drifted with him through the watery void.

At the far end of the room, she entered a tunnel and the disorientation of the illusion was released as she stumbled into clarity, in full view of everyone present. A dozen voices tittered at her faux pas, and watched through their dinner masks with condescending zeal.

"Try your best to rise above all of this," Hayden whispered, and as he leaned into her their voices echoed throughout the dining room.

"Sure," she quietly answered back, not willing to let a few strangers intimidate her. "I can get over these barely tolerable conditions, if you can get me some dinner?"

The dining table stretched out for what seemed like a mile, but in truth, only thirty or so people sat at the offering. She decided they didn't all look hostile at her presence. Some were intensely curious—mostly those of the male persuasion.

"This is a feast to celebrate my return," Hayden intimately spoke in her ear once more, and the gossip flew on wings at his action.

Jasmine was beginning to feel like she was on the red carpet with a famous beau, the way everyone regarded her and spoke behind her back.

She was seated directly to the right of my Lord Amarynn, who was at the head of the table. There was no way she could have missed the fact Cordelia was seated to his left.

"I hope you enjoyed my 'Under the Sea' introduction." Cordelia's voice sliced through the ambient noise like razor-edged tentacles. After a minute of silent and daring glances at the crowd seated near her, Jasmine realized with dismay that the lady was speaking to her.

"It was definitely fishy," she responded automatically, before her sense had an opportunity to caution her tongue.

Hayden smirked at her honest answer. He looked dashing in a dark blue coat with a gold woven collar and cuff. It looked trim and smart, like maybe it was a military jacket. By some horrible coincidence, Cordelia was also wearing midnight blue and had strands of gold threaded through her upswept hair. Once Jasmine so openly appraised her in front of the entire dinner party, the blonde haired beauty was quick to return the favor.

"That is quite a lovely gown." Cordelia nodded in her direction and Jasmine smiled gratefully for her compliment. In truth, she felt more beautiful now that she ever had in her whole life.

"You must tell me," the gilded lady across the table continued. "Where did you dig up such a pre war relic? I would have thought anything of that fashion might have been moth eaten ages ago."

"We should be thankful that some fabrics are more resistant to the hungry moth, should we not, Jasmine?" Hayden cut in before her obvious lack of response appeared awkward. "I still fondly remember the blankets at the cabin where your kindness saved my life."

At his statement, daggers flew from Cordelia's openly hostile eyes and her delicate pallor took on a heated, rosy hue. She opened her mouth to prepare a stinging retort, but was silenced as a round of applause erupted from the length of the table.

"Well done, my Lady Jasmine!" A deep cheer came from further down the line.

"We're most grateful for your assistance," a soft feminine voice said directly to her right, and Jasmine jumped slightly as a satin gloved hand rested lightly on her arm. She turned to see if the owner of such a friendly gesture might be mocking her as well, but saw only kindness and respect in the eyes of the young woman.

"And I love the style of your gown. It has been far too long since we have seen such a lovely fashion in the court," she added. "I will speak to my dress maker tomorrow and have her make one similar."

The voices of many women echoed that sentiment, and Jasmine was more grateful for the kindness than she could express. When Cordelia abruptly stood and threw down her napkin like a spoiled child, shocked whispers rocked the gathering hall once more and she was relieved not to be the focus this time.

"If you will excuse me, my Lord." She stiffly inclined her neck in Hayden's direction. "I am sure I feel quite ill, suddenly."

He rose and made a formal bow in her direction, letting her know she was dismissed from the group. The occupants of the room became as quiet as the grave at the display. No sound could be heard except the sharp click of Cordelia's heels, which echoed with an angry retort on the polished hardwood floor during her hasty and dramatic exit.

Jasmine noticed as the furious woman yanked the door open to the waiting room that the illusion was turned off and it was a drab, plain looking area without the assistance of the holographic device.

Before the door had closed entirely behind her, the crowd began chatting and the atmosphere was decidedly more relaxed with her absence.

"Where are the monks?" Jasmine leaned toward Hayden as she imitated the actions of the others around her and served herself from the banquet style platters that crowded the table. The surface was so covered by gold and silver plates, piled high with exotic looking food, that she couldn't even see the top of the table.

"They would say they were not socially suited for such functions," he answered her diplomatically. "But I think they can't stand the politics of the court, if you ask me."

"I kind of see their point." She smiled at his candid response. "Can we eat with the monks tomorrow night?"

"We may if you like." He nodded his approval at her request; "Though I have to warn you that every member of the order lives under a vow of silence, save a handful of instructors."

"So, not a lot of gossip going on over at that part of the keep," she said, and that suited her just fine.

"Oh, I don't know," he smiled. "I think you'd be surprised at how well they communicate. But every novice initiated into the order takes the vow and for seven years they do not speak a word until their training is complete. To even refer to a matter in time would be heresy and it is an ever present reminder that they must never give away their secrets."

"Well, they don't have to worry about me, then. I have nothing to tell. I really have no idea what is going on." Jasmine felt a little more comfortable as the warm food settled in her stomach.

"Oh, hey," she added, looking at Hayden, not realizing her informal address had drawn a bit of attention at their end of the table. "Can I ask you a question?"

"You may ask me anything, as you wish," he answered her, charmed and completely at ease with her unusual way of speaking to him.

A dozen ears leaned a little closer the Lord of the Manor, just waiting to hear what outrageous thing this strange woman would ask of their ruler.

"I have this girl in my room," she started hesitantly, trying to imagine the best way to put it. "I'm thinking she's probably really hungry, because I'm sure Cordelia had her chained up in the stables or something for at least a week."

There was a gasp from the far end of the table and Jasmine

leaned closer to her host before whispering loudly, "Longer than a week, if you ask me. She didn't smell all that fresh. So, can I just take this empty plate here and load it up with food? There's plenty and I can run it up to her really quick ... "

As her words fell away, she realized that every single person in the room was looking at her in amazement. Jasmine glanced at their shocked faces, and then defiantly began to spoon heaps of potatoes and carrots onto the spare tray.

"She sent you someone from the stables?" Hayden laughed, and immediately everyone joined in. "I'll make sure you have a proper serving girl in the morning."

"She is a proper serving girl," Jasmine immediately defended the child that had been so kind to her. "Besides, I'd rather have someone Cordelia didn't like, over someone she did."

"She has a point there, Edward," said the pretty young woman who took her side earlier. "This woman is quite clever! I approve."

"Edward?" Jasmine looked at him incredulously, forgetting the tray of food she was working on.

"My sister always called me by my middle name when we were children, didn't you, Meredith?" he said in what was clearly a teasing tone.

"Oh, you know I hate Meredith!"

"Be that as it may, my dear sister, it is how we addressed each other up until we were grown."

"Call me Vierna." The woman offered her recently ungloved hand to Jasmine, and she could tell that her feelings were not truly hurt. "I am pleased to meet the woman whom my brother has been speaking of every minute since his return."

"Edward?" Jasmine echoed again faintly, still looking at him with her brow furled.

"Come, my Lady," he smiled gently. "Surely that is not such an uncommon name as your own."

"No, it's fine," she answered quickly. "It's just a strange coincidence, like everything else here."

"It does not matter anyway." He laughed. "You will have to call me my Lord Amarynn in matters of State."

"Pfft." She sniffed before she thought better of it. He raised one brow and his blue eyes sparkled at her defiance.

"I'll never be in 'State,' then," she finished, and began to spoon food on the tray again.

"Somehow I think you'll be wrong about that," he whispered to himself, before he leaned forward and took the ladle from her hand.

"If your girl is trained to serve as you think," he interjected immediately as soon as she began to bristle, "she will have escorted you to the entrance and then gone directly to the kitchen to join the others. On feast days, everyone eats the same food."

"Oh," Jasmine looked down, embarrassed at the rather large stack of edibles she had scooped from nearly every platter she could reach. "That's a really nice thing to do."

"If it makes you feel better, I'll have someone go check on her, just to make sure she felt she was welcomed," he added, trying to suppress a grin as Jasmine slid the large tray in front of her and began to nibble on the huge servings she had placed there.

"I suppose that will do, for now," she said with all of the royal manner she could compose, and no one but Hayden dared to find amusement with her answer.

"If you have quite finished, my Lady, I should like to ask if you would allow me to accompany you to the garden?"

Jasmine was about to say that some fresh air would be awesome, but a few of her closest dinner companions turned eager and questioning eyes her way, and left her feeling a little nervous about the proposal.

"Um, yes, a walk would be most enjoyable?" she said, hoping that if she phrased her answer in the form of a question she might win a prize.

"Griff," Vierna instantly called from her side. Jasmine was startled by the noblewoman's excited cry, but relaxed as a harmless looking, white-haired gentleman appeared next them both. Vierna took his arm and spoke into his ear. He turned with all the surprise a pair of elderly eyes could muster behind bushy eyebrows and pressed his thick goggled glasses close to her face.

"Please note, Griff, the Lady Jasmine has agreed that a walk in the garden with Lord Amarynn would be most enjoyable."

"Ah, yes," he mumbled to himself, cracking open an old ledger he had at his side. "I remember the Lady Jasmine."

"Oh?" a voice challenged from further down the line. Many eyes turned and Jasmine was immediately aware of the skinny, pale looking fellow who had spoken the dissident words. His hair was dark and fine, thin at a glance, and she got the feeling he greased palms for a living. It didn't matter what she felt. The heir apparent didn't care to have his servant challenged.

"You dare to speak against a lifelong scribe of the court, Ference?" Hayden stood behind the table, and everyone turned to see what had gotten his ire.

"Of course not!" The limp and pasty fellow stood himself, and compulsively bowed several times to the head of the table. "I only suggest that his memory may be skewed by everything that has happened. Obviously none of us know your new friend to be a lady."

"My Lord," Hayden voice took on a formal and dangerous chill as he crossed the length of the table to reach the sorry man's location. "I know her to be a lady. If Griff says he remembers her, then he does so. His entire life is devoted to the written word and the history of my family. How dare you cast a doubt upon such a thing?"

Though it was well known to the court, Jasmine had no way of being aware of the fact that an appointed scribe could never forget a person, even if he wanted to.

The point that impressed her most was that Griff carried on as if there could never have been a question of doubt. She watched him record his entry and thought if he had been any older, his fingers might break off at the action. It was entirely possible he hadn't heard a bit of the exchange.

Hayden didn't return to his seat, but came close to Jasmine and offered her his arm. Looking around at the gallery of expectant faces, she took it as graciously as she could manage and walked slowly with him to the edge of the room.

"Why do they write down everything that happens?" she asked as they passed out of general earshot.

"They do not," her escort responded, and the dining room suddenly seemed very far behind. "Griff is a loyal scribe of the court. He is merely doing his duty."

"Okay, since you won't come right out and tell me, I have to ask what his duty is."

"He records royal events ... Marriages, funerals, courtships ..." The last word dwindled away, but it was not without courage.

"We're not married, and you're not dead," Jasmine reasoned. "Are you trying to tell me we're 'courting' like something out of an old wife's tale? Besides, you said we couldn't get our groove on until you saved the world."

"It is not as if I could tell you anything, beautiful girl, but if you're to remain with me for the time being, I have to make an honest woman of you in the eyes of the denizens of the realm," he answered and he pulled her nearer to his side. The stone corridor gave way to a dark and thickly grown tunnel of heavy, green leaves.

She felt a little prickle on her skin, as if hidden eyes watched their backs, and gladly let him hold her closer as they walked. She was more than conscious of the fact that she had let dozens of people know it was okay for him to take her to this shadowy passage to do whatever, and at least one person wrote it down.

There was a familiarity to his touch, as if he had allowed himself to be more comfortable with her now that proper protocol was being followed. She decided right then that if courtship was his game, she would play it. Even if other choices had been presented, she was intrigued by the process itself and something deep inside her soul longed to make him proud and prove herself. She had never encountered a man that made her feel this way, and she thought he was surely the match to her soul.

The heavy shadows of the trellis gave way to a garden that was probably splendid by daylight, but gave off a deeply romantic feel in the darkness. Warm colored lights glowed from within the depths of the beautifully sculpted fountains and she thought a master must have carved the life-like marble statues that sat or stood in various poses all about them. She thought that fireflies blinked off and on all over the garden, but as they came close to the lights, she saw they were tiny soft globes that floated on their own in the evening breeze. Unable to help herself, she came quite close to one with the intention of touching it. Much to her disappointment, it floated away just as she came within reach.

"For safety reasons, they are designed to move away when they sense a person is near," Hayden explained, looking with sympathy at her startled expression.

"Oh, so they don't burn anyone?" She turned to him, thinking she had the explanation right away.

"Not at all." He smiled at her reasoning, charmed by her wonder at everything that was new to her. "It is so they do not freeze anyone."

"But they look so ... warm and friendly," she gasped in spite of herself, feeling a little foolish. After all the things she had seen here, such a small item shouldn't have set her ideas on edge, but it did.

"Come with me." He pulled her away from the light that hovered just out of contact. With careful guidance, he sat her on the edge of a beautiful fountain; fine satyrs and nymphs decorated this marble reservoir also, and she had to wonder just what inspired this entire half naked, wood spirit theme they had going on. The floating globes gathered near their position, but always just at the edge of her vision.

Jasmine gazed into the water next to her, and let her hand drop aimlessly into the pool. The water was warm and inviting, just like everything else she had encountered this evening, save for a few members of the court. The reflection from the mobile luminaries painted the edges of the rippling water in fiery gold as it took its course to the very outer rim. The outwardly expanding ripple pressed out in an ever expanding ring, over and over again. The design was almost hypnotic and she leaned forward a little closer in spite of herself.

Her reflection swirled in the waves and she squinted in the dim light to see it. A pair of young, green eyes looked back at her with surprise and she drew in a sharp breath at the child like image in the water. Without realizing it, she had leaned over to the point where she was nearly touching the surface; the moment she understood that the face looking back at her was not her own, strong hands grabbed her shoulders and pulled her upright.

"Jasmine." Hayden shook her a bit sharply, in her opinion. "What do you think you're doing?"

A quick look around let her break free of the vision she had just experienced, and she noticed the ends of her hair were dripping wet.

"I was just ... " She hesitated slightly, looking around for some kind of excuse. "I was just looking at your fountain. Because it is much nicer than my fountain ... the one at my castle ... "

"What did you say?" Hayden whispered, and his supporting hands flew from her shoulders in surprise. For an instant, she nearly plunged back into the fountain at the sudden absence of pressure before she regained her balance.

"Oh man," she said, her voice confused. "I really don't know what happened there, but I strongly feel that since I have no clue, you can't be mad at me. What did I do, anyway?"

"You spoke words from my dreams," he said softly, and the look on his face was tender for a moment, as if he were remembering.

She slowly raised a finger, and with all the decorum and etiquette she could muster, jabbed him in the chest with a grin on her face.

"Does that mean I'm your dream girl?"

He briefly regarded her like she might have changed some make believe plan he had held dear for all his life, but that passed quickly and was replaced by a look that strongly indicated genuine emotion for the present.

With great care, he kneeled gently before her at the edge of her stone perch.

"Doesn't that hurt, or something?" she immediately protested, feeling very self conscious as she glanced around nervously.

"Would it be an untoward gesture for me to take your hand at this time, my Lady?" he asked, and she could tell by his tone that protocol was back on.

"If it pleases you, my Lord," she answered, trying to remember they way all the actors had spoken during the many times she had seen Camelot at the theater. As long as she stuck to some kind of formal manner, she had less chance of playing this wrong.

Hayden reached out his right hand, palm up, and she laid hers on top of it. The heat from his touch made her shiver as he took his left hand and covered hers like a precious treasure. He gazed up into her eyes and there was something so sensual, so powerfully moving in the fact that this strong, beautiful man gave her the honor of his knee.

Though the only contact they had was through the skin of their palms, she felt an overwhelming sense of passion and desire. He merely held her there, but she felt like ages stretched before her as destiny manifested itself clearly in her mind. She was losing herself in his deep blue gaze, and she didn't care if she ever came back again.

"I chose wisely," he whispered with reverence, and she felt herself falling toward his lips as the words formed. "My Lady." His voice was the merest whisper now, but nothing else was needed because she was close enough to taste his sweet breath. "It would be untoward for you to grace me with a chaste kiss."

The tiny space that separated their skin couldn't have existed as a buffer when they spoke, but somehow she couldn't reach his lips. For all she knew, the damn courtship protocol physically prevented her from moving forward.

"Chaste my Aunt Fanny," she replied, and in her mind she pushed the barrier away as she leaned forward.

The force that drew them together was undeniable, unstoppable, even God himself couldn't—

"Ah hem." A nasty little cough pierced her brain and she was forced to look at the source.

Mr. Ference, or whatever his title was, stood at the edge of a long row of rather concealing bushes—too concealing by far, if you asked Jasmine. Unfortunately, no one had.

"I have located your serving girl," he said in a complacent tone, and she got the feeling that he was definitely up to no good. Jasmine was instantly terrified that Jesi might have had to walk even as far as the covered trellis with such a slimy character.

"You will produce my girl at once," she demanded in a strong and clear tone that sounded for the entire world like a born and bred courtesan.

Like her tail was on fire, Jesi flew from the shadows and hid behind Jasmine's skirts.

Hayden gave her a surprised look, and even Ference appeared to be a bit intimidated. With a staying arm behind her back, Jasmine approached the skulking character.

"If you have done anything to harm her," she started the threat, and he shrank against her words, completely cowed.

"My Lady Jasmine," Hayden was suddenly at her side. "Ference is a member of my court, not to mention the brother of Lady Cordelia."

The thin haired man grew a little backbone at that statement, and attempted to draw himself up to his full height. He nearly reached Jasmine's chin with the effort.

"It wouldn't be proper for a lady to be courted without the presence of her girl, would it now?" he sneered, and the spark in his eye was vengeful and dangerous. Before that remark, Jasmine would have discounted him as weak and harmless. Now she knew he was mad enough to try anything.

"You're correct, indeed." Hayden bowed before him stiffly, and motioned for him to leave. Not one of them missed the satisfied smirk on his face as he slunk away and Jasmine shivered in his wake.

"He is not an enemy to be discounted, my dear," he spoke to her informally, and she was glad he didn't mince words or try to protect her sensibilities. All her life, if she was up against something, she wanted to know what it was.

The moment Ference's back faded in the distance and he disappeared into the dark tunnel of plant life, Jesi fell to Hayden's feet, crying.

"I am sorry, My Lord Amarynn." She sounded so afraid through her tears. He regarded the child with a puzzled look of half recognition, as he was trying to remember where they had met before.

"There is nothing to be sorry for, my dear." His tone was gentle as he set his hand on her shoulder in an effort to comfort her. The second he made contact with her hidden bruise she cried out in pain, spun from his touch like a whirlwind and buried her face in Jasmine's skirts.

"I gather Cordelia has not been so kind to her." Her green eyes flamed to the confused man in explanation, and she rested the palm of her hand on the child's head. In just a few moments, the crying stopped.

"That is one thing for which I hold no surprise," he answered with a frown, and motioned for her to join him at his side. Just as he predicted, Jesi fell into her role and positioned herself just behind the couple. "Perhaps I can escort the two of you to your rooms for the evening?"

She didn't miss the disappointment in his tone. She began to unclench her fists for the first time since that skinny, unpleasant man rained on her parade. With surprise, she felt a warm metal circlet at the center of her grasp and realized Hayden must have slipped the silver ring into her palm right before they were discovered.

As she began to hold it out to him, he swiftly caught the back of her hand and curled her fingers tightly around the object before anyone could see. Just ahead, as they entered the corridor, she thought she caught the shadow of a man lurking in the distance. As they drew close there was nothing there and she chalked it up to her imagination.

It probably wasn't.

♦

The sunlight fell on her face and invaded the cool, dark realm of sleep she tried to linger in. After that first experience with the dream at the cabin when she woke with Hayden holding her hand, there were no more visions of terror. Only wonderful sleep time memories of things like castles and mothers and ivory handled brushes.

As she lay curled up in the deep feather mattress, everything that had happened worked its way into her thoughts once more. She didn't panic. She closed her eyes and smelled the rich scent of the burning wood in the fireplace as the timber crackled behind the screen. A deep feeling of satisfaction set upon her soul and she thought she could lie there and think of Hayden all morning.

It always amazed her how quickly her mind could be changed, especially when the smell of freshly baked bread was becoming more and more prevalent in the room. One could only pray there was coffee. A ludicrous vision of a group of monks kneeling around a Starbucks came to mind and she laughed in spite of herself as she emerged from beneath her blankets.

Jesi was lightly humming a lovely, but sad tune as she went about her work with her back to her mistress. She set a large assortment of covered platters on a small table near the fireplace as Jasmine slipped quietly from the bed. Alerting her with a wide yawn, the girl spun about with a huge smile on her face.

"My Lady!" she breathed, her excitement barely containable. "The Lord Amarynn sent me a message in the kitchens today, and has asked for you to join him in the grand library of the Order of Darkenbane after you have eaten!"

"That sounds so … thrilling."

The girl's cheeks dimpled and she ran forward and clasped the sleepy woman in a friendly manner.

"Hey, what was that for?"

"I am just so happy for you! They say in the kitchens that Lord Amarynn will wed you before the next season," she blurted out, then covered her mouth as if she had given away a great secret.

"That kind of talk is just silly, Jesi," she answered immediately, but a part of her heart thrilled at the impossible thought and she couldn't help it.

Breakfast didn't stand a chance against her with her Prince Charming waiting on the wings. Jesi seemed to be as excited as she was, and as soon as the plates were clear she ran to the mahogany wardrobe that took up a large part of the far side of the room.

As lovely as the fine court dresses were, Jasmine found herself wishing she could just put on a pair of clean jeans and a warm sweater. The girl began to spread them out for her inspection, when she turned and saw the look on her face.

"Don't these please you?" she asked immediately in a concerned tone.

"Oh, they are all beautiful," Jasmine was quick to answer, and she meant it. "But maybe something a little more comfortable and a little less fancy would be better if I am going to visit the monks?"

She waited to see how the young girl would react to her statement, and was delighted to see a look of understanding in her eyes.

"My mother often traveled with my father in the service of the guard." Jesi practically beamed with understanding. "I could fetch you some of her traveling clothes, if you would like that."

"I would love that," she answered, and before she could thank the girl she was out the door, her footsteps fading down the hall.

◆

The leather pants were slightly short on Jasmine, but nearly the same size everywhere else; it didn't really matter at the end, because Jesi showed her how to pull the thick woolen socks up around her calves before she stepped into the soft, brown boots. A finely woven white blouse billowed at the sleeves and laced across her chest, which turned out to be very accentuated by the dark, corseted jerkin that tied up the front.

She spun around in front of the mirror, her dark hair glossy and full of lustrous curls from the oil Jesi had applied. Her legs looked shapely and graceful, and she wondered how it was possible for her traveling clothes to show more of her figure than the light, off the shoulder silk gowns of the ladies at court.

"You look beautiful." Jesi stared at her reflection in the mirror.

"Much more lovely than Cordelia."

"Hey, thanks." Jasmine laughed as she spun around once more. "How much do I owe ya?"

The girl looked at her in confusion, and then shook her head.

"I'm kidding. I meant how much do I have to pay you for the compliment," she added, hoping Jesi would understand the joke.

"But it is the truth," Jesi exclaimed, though there was a twinkle in her eye.

Jasmine grabbed her bag and felt much more comfortable carrying it around dressed as she was. She did end up feeling like she was traveling somewhere after all. The monastery was a maze of stairs and passages that seemed to stretch on for miles. It was easy to see where the royal portion of the keep ended and the modest living quarters of the monks began.

A few elaborate tapestries and rugs still appeared from time to time as they turned a corner, but she definitely got the idea that they had left the lap of luxury and entered an ancient fortress meant for functionality. She was still amazed by the mix of what seemed medieval, yet woven throughout the archaic sense was a highly advanced technology. Where there would be torches, there were softly glowing spikes of endless light. She noticed most of the technological aspects that seemed superior to those of her world were energy and illusion based comforts.

The spare, but comfortable corridor Jesi had led her through ended at a set of large wooden doors. They were not unlike the ones she came through on her arrival, minus the rusty hinges and battle scars on the darkened oak outside. With ease, the small girl pushed on the right side and it appeared to open away with no effort at all. It swept inward as if it were a giant hand, beckoning her inside and telling her she was welcome.

Her leather boots didn't make a sound on the polished stone floor as they entered, but Jesi's shoes tapped lightly enough to echo in the vast space before them. This was definitely a library, though she had never seen so many books in one place before. The shelves covered the walls for as far as she could see, and stand alone book cases lined up and down in rows to make aisles. Thick wooden tables dotted the open spaces, and there was an odd assortment of men in various states of concentration seated at most of them. Some were young, and some were old. They came in every shape, size and color and the only thing they seemed to have in common was a plain brown set of clothes that looked like a uniform to her.

"Let me guess, these are the monks?" Jasmine whispered to Jesi, who only nodded in answer.

Despite her care, she immediately drew the attention of a young man who sat at the nearest table. He looked up in shock at the sound of her voice, but then a wide grin crept across his face as he saw her. He quickly rapped on the wood with his knuckles in a strange pattern, which got the nearby monks involved also. The sound spread throughout the room very quickly and before she knew it, she had a crowd peeking at her from behind a multitude of shelves and ladders.

Though she was the object of many curious faces, only one person approached her. The young boy came forward shyly, and she saw immediately that he was no older than Jesi might have been. He wore regular clothing, but he came up to them with all the respect of a trained monk.

"Are you the Lady Jasmine?" he whispered, his deep amber eyes clearly dazzled at her presence. He had shoulder length, light brown hair that fell across his face as he blushed.

"I am." She smiled at the handsome child, trying her best to put him at ease. "I thought the monks took a vow of silence when they entered the order of Darkenbane."

"They do." A deep, rich voice answered her question and Hayden approached them from a hidden niche to the side. With a fond look on his face, he reached out and tousled the boy's hair.

"This is my distant cousin, Luke," he explained, as the child twisted out from under his hand. "He is not a member of the order, though nothing we can do will keep him out of the library!"

Jasmine turned to meet the newcomer, trying to resist the urge to throw her arms around him in front of everyone. His blue eyes smoldered as he regarded her trim figure, and his lids dropped to half mast as he appreciated her leather clad form. Though she didn't see it, the expression on Luke's young face fell as he watched the two of them together.

"I have brought you something, my Lady." Hayden had been holding one hand behind his back as he came to greet them. He withdrew a small book and she reached out to take it.

She gasped with astonishment as she looked at the fine leather tooling on the cover. It was nearly identical to the one she had inside her bag at this very moment. The infinity symbol was new and clear, not worn in any way. With shaking fingers she gently opened the supple cover to the first page. After turning a few in rapid succession, she realized all the pages were blank.

"Where did you get this?" She looked at him in wonder, feeling the thick, soft pages beneath her fingertips.

"When I saw your book at the camp, it seemed familiar to me," he explained. "When I arranged to meet you here today, I knew why. There are many of these in the back room of the library, because that is what the Watchers used to record their encounters in the other worlds. I thought you night like a brand new one to transfer the tales from your old book, as you said it was something you hoped to accomplish."

Jasmine nearly broke down then and started to tell him that there was really nothing to write, but she was so touched by the gift she didn't care to say anything.

"It's so beautiful, thank you." She slipped the new book into her travel bag.

"Jesi, could you please go to the kitchens to let them know the Lady and I will be dining with the initiates this evening?" Hayden smiled at her in such a way that Jasmine thought the girl would probably walk to the ends of the earth and bring him back his favorite poesy if he so asked. She knew she certainly would.

Her serving girl kept her quiet manners with a nod and a blush before she quickly exited through the same door they had just used.

The sun streamed through high windows, but she noticed that it didn't fall onto any of the precious books in the room. It did bathe Hayden in a warm glow, however, and his thick blonde hair glistened in the light. Her body ached with a deep need to be close to him, and as she looked into his eyes her passion must have been obvious because she saw a spark within the depths of his gaze. His thickly lashed eyelids dropped once again, and she finally realized he did it to conceal the desire that lay just beneath the surface of his restraint.

Oh my God, that is so sexy.

The moment her fingers made contact with his sleeve, the outer doors flew open and hit the side walls with a huge, resounding thud. Jasmine startled at the violence of the noise in the quiet place and immediately put her free arm protectively around the small boy who had lingered near. Her face was strong and alert as she prepared for whatever was next.

She stared straight ahead at the messenger who rushed over to them, panting and clearly flustered.

Luke stared at her lovely face in total and complete adoration.

"My Lord Amarynn," the messenger panted, really just a boy upon closer inspection, though he had a very adult look on his face. "There is a matter of urgency, which you need to attend quickly."

Hayden remained calm in the face of obvious panic, and his very attitude seemed to calm the young man a little.

"Tell me what it is," he said slowly, giving the page his full attention.

The unfortunate bearer of the news cast his glance to Jasmine, then back to his master before he finally stalled.

"You may say whatever you need to say in her presence, if that is your concern," he encouraged the boy.

"The council sends word that there has been a dimensional breach," he panted, eyes wide and afraid.

The nearest monks heard the news as well, and that strange series of taps crested through the echoing room in waves.

"Do they know where this has happened?" Hayden steadily questioned him, not even a strain of pressure on his face as he held the boy's gaze.

The page leaned very close, and Jasmine was sure she was the only other person who heard his words.

"Someone has opened an unsanctioned ring inside the monastery."

Hayden nodded, and just as she thought he was turning to her, he faced his young cousin instead.

"Would you please take the Lady into your care for a short while as I attend to matters?" He spoke to him as if he were an adult, and Luke stood as tall as he could at the request.

"I would be delighted," he answered, clearly very proud to be chosen as he stepped to her side.

"I will return shortly." Hayden came very close to Jasmine as he whispered in her ear. He pulled away, but didn't break eye contact and so he saw the look of disappointment on her face. With a mischievous smile, he bent down again and kissed her on the forehead. Even the messenger seemed stunned by his action, but Jasmine finally believed that no matter what happened, he would always come for her.

He was gone an instant later, and she thought her heart walked right out with him. After a few polite minutes, Luke stepped between her and the closed door, offering his arm very carefully in the way that he had seen Lord Amarynn do.

He led her to a table and held out a chair. She was amazed by his graceful movements and very grown-up attitude. After she was comfortably seated, he walked around and took the place opposite.

She watched him watching her, and there was no mistaking the fact that the boy was smitten. His eyes sparkled and he held the slightest flush high on his cheeks as he thought of something to say.

"May I see the book Lord Amarynn gifted you?" he inquired politely.

"Do you write in these books yourself?" she asked as she handed it over, relieved to have a topic for discussion.

"Oh no," he said, and visibly relaxed a little now that she was talking to him like a normal person. "Only the Watchers write in these. And you, I guess!"

She laughed at his clever statement, and was suddenly thankful for his company. It took her mind off what was happening with the council, though she really had no idea what the council was. Sometimes not knowing was much worse.

"What is a Watcher, then?" She wanted to ask him more serious questions, but didn't think he was really old enough to explain the intricacies of the council or their mission statement. She didn't realize how strange that query might be to someone who had lived their whole life in the realm until he gave her an odd look. Luke might as well have asked her what a president was while they were standing on the White House lawn.

"Just pretend like I don't know anything," she said with as little sarcasm as possible. After all, it really wasn't far from the truth.

"Yes, Lady Jasmine," he said, and he had such a strange tone in his voice when he spoke her name. If he were not so young, she might think he was about to utter his undying love.

After an encouraging nod, he looked around to see if anyone was listening before he began.

"There are two kinds of monks in Darkenbane," he explained. "A Watcher travels through the sliver between worlds and they record everything they see. A Sensor stays here in the realm, and reads whatever was written. Sensors have a way of seeing the future of our kingdom by studying information from the worlds that mirror ours."

"So," she said, impressed with his understanding of the order. "If you don't read the books, and you don't write in them, what exactly do you do here all the time?"

"The monks teach me to paint." He grinned with excitement, and his face took on a child like joy that was much more fitting for someone his age. He held out his hands a little shyly and she could see that he did indeed have different colors of pigment on his skin. He tucked the evidence back under the table and looked at her for a moment, his cheeks coloring once more.

"Perhaps one day you would allow me to paint you," he almost pleaded. "You're the most beautiful lady I have ever seen!"

"I'll bet you don't get around much, then."

When he continued to hold her gaze in earnest, she felt like she needed to change the subject.

"Since you do come around the books a lot, perhaps you could take a look at this old one that was left to me by my family." She fumbled around in the bag a little longer than she needed to, hoping the intensity of the child's regard would lessen. "It means a lot to me, and I would love to know more about it if you could help."

"Oh, yes." His eyes brightened at the thought she needed him. With delicate action, he reached forward and took the old book, exchanging it for the new one that she had just received. "This is very old, I think." He touched the cover with enthusiasm. "We had a lot of books styled like this, but then something happened to them. No one has written in that kind since, which I guess is why Lord Amarynn let you have one."

"What happened to them?" she asked immediately, remembering that Hayden had mentioned something once about finding the lost prophecies of his people.

"I don't really know." Luke shrugged. "But this is the first one like it that I have ever seen used up, even if the ink is faded."

He was obviously fascinated by the object, and Jasmine's head filled with a lot of questions that she couldn't hope he'd have answers for. That was why neither of them noticed the second messenger to enter the library that day.

"Lady Jasmine," he spoke crisply, and she looked up to see an older gentleman dressed in black and silver. He had some kind of crest on his tabard, and she noticed out of the corner of her eye that Luke made a face when he recognized it.

She nodded at him, because she didn't think her voice would be very friendly if she spoke to him at the moment. He seemed really creepy, in a polished sort of way.

"My Lord Amarynn has asked me to escort you to his ready room. Something of importance has occurred and he feels you should be brought to him safely, with all haste."

She instantly thought of the trouble earlier when he had left her so abruptly and worry overrode her good sense as she sprung to her feet, tossing the bag over her shoulder.

"What are we waiting for?"

He gave her a slick and disquieting glare. He motioned her to his side with a black velvet gloved hand, and she was unaccountably relieved when he didn't touch her in any way.

She was down the corridor so fast she was immediately lost and at the mercy of her guide. In her haste, she had forgotten she left the child back at the table, holding her book. He hadn't forgotten Jasmine, however, and trailed her as quickly as he could with the leather bound treasure clutched tightly to his chest.

She could tell they reentered the royal quarters by the décor alone, even before they began to pass servants and courtesans in the hall. They hastily turned a corner, where she nearly collided with a man traveling just as quickly as she was.

"Oh, I'm sorry," she automatically apologized, holding out her hand to make amends. When she looked up she met the scowling gaze of Ference, whose pale fingers fluttered nervously in front of her.

Her guide nodded to the agitated man briskly, and she noted that Ference did the same. Cordelia's brother was dressed in black again, with silver trim along his cuff. It struck her as a little odd that the two fellows matched, but she was impatient to reach Hayden and help him in any way that she could.

Just a few steps past Ference, the messenger opened a thick lacquered door so highly polished that she could see her reflection in it. Nearly out of breath from her stint through the monastery, she rushed in.

For a moment, she couldn't really understand that the only person in the room was Cordelia. Apparently even her guide disappeared and she was utterly alone with the woman.

"Where is Hayden?" she demanded, not even trying to keep her dislike for the vindictive woman out of her voice. With a cautious eye, she noted that Cordelia stood very near a ring on the wall and there was no doubt it was active.

"He was forced to go ahead," she answered smoothly, so perfectly devoid of emotion that Jasmine had no way to sense her intent. "He asked me to assure your passage behind him and I gave him my word that I would."

"I don't think so." Jasmine clenched her teeth. Both women were so focused on each other that neither saw Luke slip through a crack in the door, wide-eyed at the spectacle.

Cordelia regarded her with cold disdain, and snapped her fingers one time. The room seemed to shift beneath her feet for one disorienting second, and she found she was facing away from the manipulative courtesan instead of standing in front of her as she had thought.

When the room shifted, Luke found himself behind a tapestry, but he wasn't fooled for a minute. With quick fingers, he poked through the illusionary fabric and opened his mouth to warn Jasmine.

It was too late.

She walked across the room and reached for what she thought was the door handle, but was actually the surface of the ring.

In that very instant she was gone.

Cordelia laughed in triumph, and snapped her fingers once again. The room wobbled briefly and exposed Luke as he stood against the wall in terror.

Like a swift bird descending upon her prey, the wicked woman flew across the room and grabbed him by the jaw with her sharp fingers. Tears streamed from his eyes and his hands reflexively held up the book he was cradling so carefully.

"If you speak of this to anyone, Lucas Amarynn, I shall cut out your tongue." Her voice was so filled with hate and menace that he trembled as her fingers bruised his jaw. "And don't think of helping her, either. That was a one-way passage and it's about time she went back to where she came from."

She let go and he collapsed onto the stone floor in anguish, sobbing like his heart was broken. Cordelia hummed a little tune as she circled the ring with her fingers. When it reached the smallest size, she flung it carelessly into the brightly burning coals of the marble fireplace. The moment the flames sparked, she turned on the child once more with a devious look on her face.

"Pull yourself together and pack you bags." She bent down over his figure, which instinctively became still as her icy shadow fell over him. "Tonight you enter the glorious Order of Darkenbane, and never a word will you be able to speak of this again upon penalty of death."

•

She hit her head this time for sure. It was an iron lamp post, she thought, at least as far as she was able to make out through her hazy vision. Her gaze was drawn upward to the flickering flame, but it didn't appear to be electric. In fact, she was sure that gas hissed through the opening of the partially enclosed lantern at the top.

It was getting dark and as she struggled to stand, a horse and carriage almost ran her down as they careened madly around the corner. She held on tight and allowed the post to stop swaying before she decided to let it go and stand on its own.

All the people who had been on the street a moment ago were rapidly clearing out and she was a little concerned by that fact. A row of strong, muscular men were paraded by with no shirts on, weighed down by heavy barrels of brick and mortar on their shoulders. Their dark skin glistened in the fading light, and she noticed that they carefully looked away from her.

"Honey, are you alright?" The feminine voice was distant in her ears and she reached out for her friend the lamp pole one more time while she tried to focus.

"I don't mean to scare you, honey." The woman sounded a little more persistent this time. "But it's no good for you to be standing on the street at night, especially dressed like that. The sailors will land soon and when they don't find brides, they come lookin' for us."

"Where am I?" She turned bleary, unfocused eyes on the pretty blonde stranger who began to tug a little desperately on her sleeve.

"You're in the Crescent City, near to Canal Street! Lord Almighty." She crossed herself nervously and detached Jasmine's fingers from the rapidly cooling metal she had been clinging to.

She was in the New Orleans, alright ... And from the look of things, it was New Orleans about a century ago.

Chapter Eight

She knew there were still carriages that roamed the quarter in her time, but Jasmine highly doubted there were ancient motor cars sputtering down the brick laid streets, so her suspicions about the date were confirmed as she leaned heavily on the small woman who hurried her along. She glanced up at a signpost in the gloom of twilight and saw the words "Basin Street" along one side.

The houses were rather stately, and even as she struggled along trying to remember just what exactly happened, the thick panes of glass on the front of the structures began to glow with welcoming warmth.

"Here we are, honey." The tiny blonde urged her up a set of stone stairs. She gave Jasmine an apprehensive glance when she opened the dark oak door at the top like she almost expected her to balk at the entrance, but upon seeing no reaction, led her in. The thickly leaded glass inside the wood sparkled in the lamp light of the foyer when the door swung closed, and the petite girl began to propel her quickly to a set of wooden stairs at the opposite end as if she were afraid they would be seen.

A low whistle came from the doorway of an open room to the right just as they passed. Her escort froze, and then drew a deep breath before she swiveled to look inside.

The word "parlor" sprung immediately to the disoriented woman's mind. There were several pieces of furniture that looked like works of art to Jasmine—all polished, carved wood with plush, velvet cushions. Gilded frames that supported heavy mirrors hung on the rich golden striped wall paper, along with numerous silk tapestries and paintings.

Curiosity got the best of her and she advanced slightly into the doorway, far enough to see an old absinthe bar in the corner.

"Look what the cat dragged in. What have ya got there, Candyce?" A friendly, melodic voice spoke from a secluded alcove just inside.

Reluctantly, the woman gently urged her into the opulent room with a sigh on her lips.

"If this is a new girl, you be gettin' a bonus for sure!" He smiled with perfect white teeth, and blew a light tune on his saxophone.

Jasmine realized there were three men gathered in the corner, all of them holding instruments and appeared to be preparing for a show.

Candyce looked a little rattled by his question. It was possible she was asking herself why she had helped some strange woman she found lying on the curb. Jasmine watched her with interest, curious herself, as she also tried to think of a reason.

"This is ... my sister, come from Boston," she said hesitantly while she decided if that excuse would do. "And she's not for the trade, I'll have you know!"

"Then what is she about, dressed like that at night on Basin Street?" He laughed, but his tone was harmless and it was difficult to feel any hostility toward him. His sweet and gentle look faded immediately, however, as his glance fell behind her shoulder to the doorway they had just come through.

Jasmine didn't need to be told that her guard should be up. The prim and proper posture assumed by the musicians spoke volumes about what she needed to know. The scent of lilac reached her senses before she could consider a plan, and her new friend plastered on a wide, terrified smile before she turned her charge around with a tight grip.

She steeled herself for a fearsome foe. Her scattered mind conjured strange images of the things she and Hayden had faced during the past few days to remind her that you never knew what could happen.

"Welcome to my house," the elderly woman spoke kindly, with a long southern drawl. Her blue haired wig was swept up in a graceful coil on top of her wrinkled forehead, and the light purple eye shadow on her thin skin almost looked like a bruise. Almost.

This new terror looked for all the world like somebody's grandma headed for church on a Sunday morning to put a few dollars on the collection plate. Jasmine knew better than anyone that looks could be deceiving, and the sharp pressure from Candyce's fingertips on her arm reaffirmed that notion.

"May I present my sister, Miss Lulu," the small woman began courageously. "Come from, from—"

"From Boston." Jasmine smiled confidently, completely aware her clothes and her manners were the farthest thing from acceptable you could get in the South at the turn of the century. Maybe that would lend credence to this spotty "out of town" tale that was born from accident and necessity. Either way, she intended to play along until she could figure out what happened.

"Such a strange accent, for Boston," the shrewd woman pointed out immediately, but it didn't rattle Jasmine after all the things she had faced down recently.

"I am well traveled," she shot back assuredly, and somewhere from the alcove she heard a strangled cough at her daring remark.

"Perhaps you would be willing to escort an old woman to her table, while we have a drink?" Miss Lulu framed the statement in the form of a question, but it was obviously a demand that couldn't be denied as she gestured to one corner that contained a table with serving ware.

The dark mahogany walls behind them held an astonishing selection of black and white photographs, many of which showed poignant, but lovely displays of a handful of women in different states of undress. There was something about them that moved Jasmine, a beauty and sadness that seemed forever lost in time. She had to remind herself that "time" was the issue here, and nothing but getting back to Hayden was more important. She was almost beside herself when she considered what he might think of her abrupt disappearance. Though her head pounded unmercifully to a chaotic beat, she had to carefully think of the events that lead her to this place. And to do that, she would have to placate the woman of the house.

"Make us a beverage, Candyce," she spoke superiorly over her shoulder at the woman who stood where she had left her. "After all, it's what you do here."

"Yes, Miss Lulu," she answered quietly, going behind the old absinthe bar in apparent defeat.

One by one the women filtered into the parlor. At first Jasmine was amazed by their beautiful satin dresses, their fine make up and hair styles. It wasn't long, however, before the ribbons came undone and the liquor flowed freely throughout the room.

Something in the back of her mind nagged at her memory, and she could recall the brief synopsis she read of the Red Light District in New Orleans in the early 1900s. She almost laughed to herself when she realized she was in a brothel, until she understood the reason Lulu was so friendly to her.

She was a little dizzy by that point, and it was hot in the room with so many people inside. The strange show of lust and desire that played out in front of her only served to remind Jasmine's senses of what she had left behind and spark a longing in her soul for her lost companion.

More than one eager suitor gave her an appreciative glance as they entered the establishment, and as the evening wore on the look in Miss Lulu's eye grew heavier with greed, and perhaps a little envy as well.

At first the girls ignored her completely, as if she was invisible, but when they started drinking she got a few hostile gazes. Jasmine put on a big display of swallowing down the tumblers of amber liquid Candyce placed before her, and it hadn't taken much for her to realize that her drinks were watered down to the point of being as harmless as possible.

Satisfied that Jasmine was just where she wanted her, Miss Lulu stood with her cane and crossed the room to part a heavy curtain at the rear of the parlor. A thick cloud of greasy smoke wafted out of the small area; as soon as it hit her, her vision blurred and a rush of euphoria nearly lifted her throbbing head off her shoulders. Several people joined the elderly hostess, and Candyce was instantly at her side the moment the curtain closed.

"I am so sorry," she said, wringing her hands. The music slowed to a crawl and she looked up at the woman who had tried to help her. She wanted to tell her it was okay, that after everything she had been through this was nothing, but her tongue was thick and the words stayed in her head. She still had enough sense to wonder what they were smoking in that room.

"I was just trying to help you. You're so beautiful, like the woman in the painting. I had to try to get you off the street before something far worse happened."

"What painting?" Fortunately, Jasmine had only sipped at her diluted drinks all evening; she should not be intoxicated, but the smoke alone made her woozy from that brief contact and it was difficult to gather her thoughts to speak those words.

Candyce glanced quickly around the room as a small burst of laughter came from behind the heavy drapery. She looked to her friend with the saxophone. He peered close to the curtain and then nodded briefly, his eyes wide and nervous.

The tiny blonde ducked underneath Jasmine's arm, a lot stronger than she looked. Without so much as a sound, she was lifted to her feet and the disoriented girl willingly let herself be escorted from the parlor. A few boos and hisses came from the gentlemen lounging on the various couches, but their women were quick to silence them. They didn't want Jasmine's beauty lingering to compete with theirs any more than she wanted to be present among them.

Once Jasmine was away from the overly warm and hazy room, her head began to clear.

The cool shadows of the foyer were a welcome change and she lingered in the darkness a moment to catch her breath. Candyce seemed to understand, and watched over her shoulder for anyone who might follow.

"They'll be in the opium room for hours," Candyce said in a voice that was meant to be reassuring, but came out with a tense ring. "With any luck, she won't remember you were here to begin with."

"If you don't get her put away right now, we'll all be headin' for the streets." The friendly saxophone player came out of the shadows like he had been a part of them just a moment before. "Miss Lulu is in her room makin' deals with a few richies for your sister's honor right now."

Despite herself, Jasmine laughed and the two frightened people turned to her in bewilderment.

"Everyone is so worried about my honor." Her words were still slightly slurred, a testament to the effects of small amounts of watery absinthe and second-hand smoke. "I couldn't even get Hayden to take it away. I doubt I'm in any danger."

"Honey," Candyce said in a resolute manner. "You ain't seen nothin' yet. Now get up those stairs. You can stay in my room."

Jasmine began to climb the dark mahogany steps, when she turned around at the last minute and held out her hand to the musician that had been so helpful.

He gave her a questioning look, but carefully took her offering.

"Thank you," she said sincerely, and Candyce smiled with approval at her action. "I don't even know your name."

"Why, it's Marcus, ma'am. Thank you for asking." His eyes glistened with emotion and he shook her hand with a hearty grasp.

Just as she reached the top of the stairs, the sound of heavy footsteps and voices echoed off the wood in the foyer. She immediately recognized the sound of Lulu's voice, but it was filled with displeasure.

"What do you mean she has taken ill?" Her shrill question cut through the darkness. Neither woman dared to move a muscle for fear of discovery.

"Lordy, ma'am." Marcus's voice carried up the stairwell in a pleading tone. Jasmine realized he spoke in a slightly different manner around the mistress of the house. "We has to make sure it ain't the malaria."

Deep, mumbled protests erupted from the bottom of the stairs and Jasmine smiled to herself at Marcus's ingenuity. She never would have thought of anything so clever, and the threat of malaria was very real in the swampy canal city of New Orleans that time of year.

"Keep her away from the other girls." Lulu's commanding voice bounced off the walls. "She can stay in her sister's room. Candyce only serves the drinks. Lord knows we can stand to lose her. And call in Miss Marie to burn the Juniper bundles and cleanse the house."

Her last few words sounded muffled, like a handkerchief had been placed over her nose and mouth. The sound of the front door banging open and closed went on for a few minutes as they crept closer to the bartender's room.

"I'm here in the back on the second floor," the petite woman whispered as they slipped along the corridor, going as fast as they could without making too much noise. "Miss Lulu doesn't quite make me sleep with the servants, but she let me have the old wardrobe room at the end of the hall."

"So, you're not one of the girls, then?" Jasmine inquired as politely as possible. If her new friend was a "Fancy Lady," she certainly didn't want to offend her.

"Lord Almighty, no!" she exclaimed in mock horror. "My mother would turn over in her grave at such a thing ... Even if we knew who she was."

It took all of Jasmine's restraint not to laugh out loud at her statement. She understood very well what it was like to be an orphan, and admired this woman more and more as the evening went along.

They reached the end of the long corridor without incident and as Candyce opened the door and motioned for her to enter, her heart felt a longing pang for Hayden's company. But she couldn't allow herself to be despondent over their separation. What happened was unfair, to be sure, but she had to remain strong and in control if she were to find a way back to him. She was positive he would come for her as he promised; however, there was no harm in getting out there and helping the process along if she could.

Aside from the tiny blue glow of a pilot light at the other end of the room, the space was completely dark. She stood still as her new friend moved around by familiarity, muttering under her breath and shuffling through her belongings.

"Blast, where did I put that lamp light tool? I know I left one at the door on my way out tonight."

The sound of clinking glass came from across the room and Jasmine heard the delicate hiss of the gas that must have been piped through the entire house. For a moment she nearly reached into her bag to pull out the matchbook from the airport, but instantly realized that could cause a lot of problems. It was probably best no one saw at least half the things she had in there. She didn't know what the burn policy was for witches in the early 1900s and had no intention of finding out.

A warm glow finally emanated from the corner of the room and she was struck by how similar the newly lit gas lamp was to the many antique fixtures that dotted the walls in the book shop. No wonder she hadn't been able to find a light switch in there at the time.

"We have electricity wired into the kitchen, but that's all," Candyce explained as she went to the other lamps fixed strategically around the area. "Miss Lulu doesn't like what she calls 'false light,' but I think she doesn't like to see herself so well in the mirror."

"Well, I can't say I blame her there," Jasmine answered absently, looking around the comfortable room as the soft illumination began to penetrate the remaining darkness. The blonde girl came to the shadows at the foot of the bed and set the last flame aglow. She turned and smiled widely at her new guest, but a look of concern replaced her friendly glance as she caught Jasmine's stunned reaction.

"That's the picture I told you about," she explained in a hurry, seeing the cause of her visitor's fixation. "The one that reminded me of you when I saw you for the first time on the street."

Jasmine knew her mouth was open and the skin on her face was numb as she stared at the beautiful creature in the painting. It was the same painting that hung in her shop when she first used the brass key and discovered the fountain that fateful night, though it was much less covered in dust.

Without ages of grime to coat the surface, there was no doubt she was the woman in the portrait.

"Where did you get this picture?" Jasmine whirled around so quickly that the girl was speechless for a moment as she grabbed her by the shoulders.

Instantly becoming aware of the surprise on Candyce's face, not to mention she happened to be looming over the petite woman with what must have been a crazed look, she let go quickly and took a step back to clear her thoughts.

Relief flooded her entire body and she sat down abruptly on the bed. Though she hadn't admitted it to herself before that very moment, she'd been extremely worried she might have lost all of her connections to Hayden in this strange new place. Now that she was here in this room with a familiar piece of the puzzle, she knew she had a chance to make her way back to him.

"Hey, it's okay." Her forgiving new friend sat next to her, putting a comforting arm around her. Jasmine was grateful for the supporting gesture and began to relax for the first time since she had entered the strange house. "He sells his paintings down by the French Market on Sundays," she remarked in a soothing tone, still patting Jasmine on the back. "They all look like you, all the things he paints. I saved my money for a month to buy this one."

A cold chill passed over Jasmine's body, and she shivered from the base of her spine to the nape of her neck as her stomach turned with half realization.

"What is the name of the artist?" she whispered, her skin drained of color as she looked carefully into the blonde woman's blue eyes.

"You mean you don't know?" Candyce laughed with a superior smile. "What I wouldn't give to have such a handsome, secret admirer, then."

"Please tell me." Jasmine encouraged her, the fingers on her hands trembling despite her attempt to calm them.

"His surname is foreign, or something, I can never remember it," Candyce answered obligingly. "But his first name is signed on everything he paints. See there?"

She slipped off her shoes and stood on the bed, pointing a delicate finger to the corner of the lovely frame.

"It says Lucas."

Chapter Nine

"I have to go see him right now!" Jasmine burst into motion, grabbing up her bag and making for the door. A wave of dizziness washed over her body, and she was forced to take a minute to steady herself. The blood had rushed to her head from the sudden movement and she was once again reminded she could possibly be injured a little.

Her pulse throbbed forcefully through her skull, and she lifted her hand to the pinnacle of the pain. A large knot greeted her gently probing fingertips, and she sighed.

"That's gonna be a goose egg, for sure." Candyce nodded to her with sympathy, and Jasmine didn't fight her when she pulled her back toward the bed. The petite beauty walked over to the gas fireplace and took a towel off a nearby hook. With swift and practiced movements, she crossed the room with a steaming iron kettle in her blanketed grip and poured hot water into a wash basin.

"We need to get you cleaned up, and I have to get back downstairs before anyone comes looking for me." She dipped a clean white cloth into the bowl and Jasmine couldn't help but remember the night at the cabin where she had tended Hayden's wounds. She thought she would give anything to be back there with him again.

Kneeling gently on the mattress next to her sitting patient, Candyce parted her thick hair and worked over the wound as easily as she could. Jasmine barely noticed her tender care, she was still so stunned by one overwhelming thought ...

Is Lucas the same man I met the first night I arrived in New Orleans?

She stopped asking herself how these things could be possible a long time ago, and she also planned to buy stock in Fate when she got back home; there was no way it didn't exist, and every coincidence she had faced up until this point turned out to be part of a bigger picture.

Candyce popped the lid off a canister of awful smelling salve, and Jasmine was instantly and unpleasantly brought back to her senses.

"I don't think I want that in my hair," she said stubbornly, but her hostess didn't give her any choice.

"You'll be glad I put it on in the morning." She scooped out what seemed to Jasmine like an overly large amount. "Besides, if I have to touch it, you have to wear it."

She really couldn't refute that logic and tried to ignore the pressure as it was applied. It burned at first, followed by a numbing cool sensation that settled over her scalp.

Candyce washed her hands repeatedly in the basin, but the pungent scent lingered on her skin and she laughed as she doused her fingers with rose water.

"Lord knows it isn't safe for two women to be wandering around the streets at night when the sailors are in port," she said firmly to her guest. "I think I told you that already. Besides, we won't catch him until Sunday at the market. Where do you think he's going to go before then, anyway?"

"It isn't where he's going to go that I'm worried about," Jasmine answered her with a sour face. "It's when."

"He's been living here all these years for a reason. I don't think he'll be leaving until he gets what he came for." She nodded wisely as she smoothed her light colored hair in the mirror. "And I have a feeling I know what that is."

Exhaustion was taking over, and no matter how much she wanted to head out onto the streets and fight a bunch of sailors ninja-style on her way to the market, she knew her aching head and tired muscles wouldn't allow it—not to even mention that Ninja school was always on her to do list, but she'd never quite gotten around to it.

"I guess you're right. It wouldn't be open now anyway. I don't suppose I'm lucky enough for tomorrow to be Sunday?" she asked Candyce hopefully, watching the lovely woman as she finished powdering her face and reapplying some lipstick.

"As Fate would have, Ma Cheri, it is." She smiled with her freshly painted lips in the gas light. This was the first time her Creole accent slipped past her tongue. Jasmine found it to be utterly charming and instantly felt she could trust this unique woman who saved her from the street.

With a wink Candyce was out the door, pulling it closed behind her with a silent motion. The soothing hiss of the warm gas was a surprising and comforting companion as Jasmine leaned against the wall directly underneath her portrait. If she had to wait until the morning, she would at least be productive about it. The last thing that Hayden had given her was that beautiful book, and she didn't intend to let it go to waste.

The only thing she had to write with was a feeble pen that they gave her at the bank just weeks before, but it was better that than nothing. She opened the first page of the stiff leather bound volume and ran her fingertips over the soft fiber of the paper. It felt like cloth, the surface was so supple and thick. That initial page seemed sacred to her somehow, and she decided she didn't want to make a mark on that one. So she turned to the second before she applied the ballpoint … Nothing.

In school, she might have scribbled on the margins to get the ink flowing, but that was not even a consideration here. She took out the old matchbook and opened the flap, drawing wide circles of impatient strokes until it came from the pen in a smooth and steady stream. She quickly switched back to the book.

The Fountain, by Jasmine Daye. A history of the absurd, a journal of the lost, and a tale that is sure to rival *Hitchhiker's Guide to the Galaxy …*

"Well, that part isn't quite certain yet." She laughed out loud. She thought she should begin with the letter and the key. It seemed somehow fitting for her to tell her tale in this time and place, only a century away from her starting point. The only real question was whether anyone would believe that it was a century before.

She began the story from the moment she met Lucas on the street and turned the heavy brass instrument in the rusty lock as the dark green paint fluttered down around her like a shower from the past. She took comfort that her adventure was written down, even if it was in a small book that no one would ever see.

Whether she knew it or not, just reliving those amazing moments with Hayden on paper made her feel a measure of closeness to him that no amount of self assurance could accomplish. A colleague of hers at the university had told her that a world, once written, existed forever in a dimension that was real somewhere. She didn't think he often traveled to other dimensions to test this fact, but there was no way that her own experience didn't happen somewhere. *When* it happened was something she couldn't even wrap her head around right now. Either way, that place was something she had to get back to, and fast. How tangible it was for others to believe didn't mean a lot to her at the moment.

It had only been cresting twilight when Candyce pulled her from the street and they took that short walk to the bordello where she served drinks, but Jasmine felt like days had passed since she stood in the Darkenbane Library and Hayden had gazed on her with his deep blue eyes.

Do you get jet lag from a time portal? she wondered to herself as the pen grew heavy in her hand. If she had to make an estimate, she only sat in the parlor for two hours at best, but the smoke from the secluded niche and the weak drinks took their toll. It seemed as if she had only scribed in the journal for a short while as the room grew hot from the gas lights, but flipping back through the ink stained pages she realized she must have lost track of the time.

I'll just lay my head down on the pillow for a moment. She slipped the book inside her travel bag. Her hand lingered inside the purse, and she allowed her fingers to feel their way to the small, hidden pocket inside the lining. The zipper was tiny, and the hem along the top covered it discreetly. There wasn't a lot of room for anything more than a driver's license and a few dollars in case of emergency, but she carefully felt along the interior until her touch settled on the one thing far more valuable than money.

She pressed her palm against the silver ring Hayden had so secretly passed into her possession on the last night they were together. She wanted to remove it from its hiding place so desperately, but she had no way of knowing who might come through that door at any moment. It wasn't even like a stranger would know the plain, silver piece of jewelry to be a time traveling device from another world, but as long as she did, she would be nervous about it.

Jasmine gathered the purse and held it against her chest

like a child might do with a teddy bear. It was probably just her imagination, but she thought she could feel the warmth from the ring in its secret place, and smiled as she remembered the way her heart soared when he had placed his hand against hers. She didn't have any proof, but felt sure as long as she kept his ring in her possession they would be connected in some way she could depend upon.

She struggled to stay awake, to send him a message with her thoughts even though she felt a little silly doing it. In the end, Jasmine decided she was never so worldly and knowledgeable that she could assume she knew how everything worked in the universe. Maybe she didn't need proof. Maybe if she put a little faith in Destiny, an onslaught of miracles could begin.

Either way, she was stubbornly sure of the one thing that she did believe in: Her feelings for Hayden were so strong and true, that there had to be a little magic in there somewhere.

◆

"Best get up now, miss." The sweet voice spoke to her unconscious mind urgently.

Her eyelids were heavy and resisting, though the small crack she managed to open didn't really shed any light on the subject because it was still dark out and nothing was lit in the room but the fireplace. Her head ached a little despite the care Candyce had given her, and it seemed like a lot of work to figure out what was going on just at the moment.

"I gave at the office," she mumbled into her sleeve, turning over to escape the urgent presence of the man next to her. She thought she was off the hook, until she heard the glass on the lamps clinking as he lit each one.

"It's now or never," he said with one last burst of energy, daring to grab her arm and give her a little shake.

That was all she needed to sit up and take a look around. Candyce was laying next to her, curled into a tiny ball, wearing the pretty blue satin pants and jacket she had on the day before. The darkness was rapidly giving way to the sunrise now, and she could feel it as much as see the creeping light along the window pane.

Marcus sat next to the bed, his knuckles on her arms white with stress, though he took care not to hurt her in any way. When he saw that she was fully awake, he stood and motioned for her to rouse her friend.

There was no need, because Candyce was already stirring from the commotion.

"Everyone is asleep," Marcus whispered. "If you leave now, you can make it all the way 'cross town before anyone notices."

Right on cue at the end of his words, the morning sun burst through the thick window and a stream of sweet light fell on Candyce like a halo.

"Thank you," the blue satin clad woman said with sincerity. She reached out and gently kissed Marcus on the cheek. He instantly reacted, throwing his hand up to his smooth skin, but the look on his face was thrilled and filled with wonder.

The gifted saxophone player stood back as if he were waiting for the roof to fall in from the kiss, but quickly found a more useful occupation just trying to stay out of the way as the two women jumped up from the confines of the bed and scampered around the room getting ready to leave.

"It's an adventure, Marcus." Candyce grinned, unbuttoning her jacket to reveal a lacey white corset as she quickly washed in the basin near the fire.

The skin on his cheeks darkened and he turned his face away, but not before Jasmine saw the glimmer in his eyes as he regarded her petite friend. She didn't know how she could have missed it before, but Marcus was clearly in love with the light haired beauty who dressed in a new dark velvet suit right in front of them. That realization only served to remind her of her own feelings for Hayden, and she felt an urgent need to get back to the place where he was before it was too late.

They swept through the upper floors of the mansion, less careful than they might have been without the knowledge no one who lived in the house would be up and about at that hour. When both women collided with a cloaked figure in the lower stair, Jasmine thought their carelessness had done them in for sure.

"Shh." A whisper came from the foreign woman's lips, like the silky caress of a stocking on delicate skin in the middle of the night. The strange figure held a tightly wound bundle of burning sticks and herbs in the hall.

She was elegant and stately, her skin a beautiful mixture of dark and light. Jasmine took a step back in alarm at their encounter, but

Candyce came forward to give her a kiss on the cheek.

"Marie," she breathed softly. "Thank you for coming to us."

The woman was slender and tall, perhaps taller than Jasmine herself, but her beauty was astonishing. She bent her neck gracefully to Candyce as if she were offering secrets of the highest importance to impart.

"Dis one you must fight for, Cherie," she whispered in her ear.

"I already done that, Miss Marie," the blonde whispered back.

"Time for us to take a Sunday stroll, then?" The lovely woman in the white gown turned to the captivated audience of three. "What you waiting for?"

As they left the now quiet establishment, a cool fog hung around the ground at the base of the buildings and Jasmine was struck by how little the quarter had changed in over a century. If you took away the beads and the huge skyscrapers across Canal Street, it almost looked the way she left it.

They crossed alleys of brick and pavement, but she was mostly interested in the byways that resembled the streets of her time. When Rue Royal came into view, she stopped with the sudden image of Hayden's face in the secluded courtyard when he opened his eyes for the first time and looked at her.

"Do you think you can find me a certain place on this street?" Jasmine had halted their progress at the crossing and Candyce turned to regard her with interest.

"Where do you want to go?" She obliged, aware that the market was at least an hour away from set up this early in the morning and any side-trip wouldn't be an inconvenience at this point.

When Jasmine spoke the number from memory, Candyce nodded and they turned slightly to the west.

"You want the antique district, then," she murmured with a curious look on her face, but none of them questioned her as they made their way down the picturesque street.

The blocks were very short, but with no tall buildings in the distance she couldn't gauge just how far they had gone. She looked over her shoulder at Marcus and Marie once or twice and realized they might have been related, they looked so alike. She hid an instant smile when she caught him looking fondly at Candyce's back as they walked along.

They slowed when they reached the block that housed her

range of numbers. The gated, narrow walkway that had led to the shop in her time was now a wide and open alley. A long, slender flat must have been built either as a stand alone store later on, or more likely an extension for an already existing building and taken up this extra space. But for now, empty carts and stands lined the spacious alley with the rugged brick pavement and it was definitely designed for people to walk through and do their shopping.

Even as she stood there, an elderly woman shuffled out with an armload of freshly cut flowers and arrangements, which she proceeded to stack on a table closest to the main street. She looked up long enough to glance at the strange assortment of people standing at the entrance of the mall; finally deciding they weren't customers, she flashed them a toothless grin and ambled back the way she had come.

Jasmine waited until the old woman was out of sight, then motioned for her friends to follow. Sounds of a waking city were beginning to carry on the crisp morning air and Jasmine suppressed another feeling of déjà vu as they entered the courtyard and saw a tightly knit group of shops just opening their doors and preparing their wares.

She knew it was there before she even looked. She knew the paint would be fresh and green and that the glass would sparkle in the sunlight, but she didn't know what she was going to do about it. She had carelessly left the envelope with the deed behind when she went through the fountain. Her heart pounded in her chest as she slipped her hand inside the travel bag and found the heavy brass key that had made it through everything with her so far.

Deciding to take extra careful precautions before entering the doorway, she boldly walked up to the front window and peered in the glass, hands cupped around her face to shield it from the morning light. Her mouth dropped open and fogged up the glass as she saw the familiar setup of tables and chairs in the front room.

"Maybe we better check that knot on your head again," Candyce said from the courtyard, her tone a little concerned as Jasmine moved to the door.

She didn't answer her worried friend, but held up the brass instrument instead.

"You're saying that key goes to this store?" the blonde asked skeptically, but stepped up to join her friend. If she was intent on going in there, she wasn't going to let her do it alone.

Jasmine closed her eyes and exhaled as she slipped the key into the lock, thinking that this was how it all began. This was where she saw Hayden for the first time and learned that there really was a rabbit hole to go down. With strong fingers and a stronger resolve, she turned it quickly.

A weighty clunk echoed as a metal bar let down inside, and she turned the knob above the plate. The door swung open with ease, and a feeling of nervous exhalation swept through her veins. She turned to her friend with an apprehensive smile.

"After you, since you know what you're doin'," Candyce quipped, sweeping her arm in a welcoming gesture. Marcus came very near the doorway and stood as if he were guarding a post, while Marie drifted around the courtyard without concern.

Go on in. It's not like you've never been here before! After all, she did have the deed to the shop, even if she couldn't put her hands on it at the moment.

For one second she imagined Hayden might be inside, waiting for her at the only place he knew to find her. That thought propelled her through the door and smack into the middle of the room before she remembered she should probably be cautious. Candyce was right behind her, but both women froze as the sound of boots echoed off the floor boards in the adjacent library.

Jasmine's heart squeezed painfully in her chest and she didn't dare to even hope it could be her wayward prince approaching. The door between the two rooms swung open and a small, darkly clad man entered; he was holding a ledger of some type and muttering to himself in distraction. After a minute of quiet pondering, the girls decided they weren't in any terrible amount of danger.

Jasmine's foot involuntarily tapped on the blonde hardwood floor with impatience and disappointment. She immediately stopped the moment it happened, but it was too late. She braced herself for a bevy of hostile questions, such as, "How the hell did you get into my store?" But nothing like that occurred.

"There you are," the studious man exclaimed in delight, looking up from the page and pushing his little round rimmed glasses back up onto the bridge of his nose.

"Here I am," she answered carefully, not willing to give anything away until she knew what was going on.

"We have been expecting you for such a long time now." He seemed truly happy to see her and stumbled over the leg of a chair in front of him in his excitement to reach her. He held his ledger clasped to his chest with his left hand and held out his right for her to take.

Out of habit alone, she shook it and was surprised by his strong, warm grasp.

"I sent my wife on ahead, dearest Millie," he began talking all at once, as if he expected her to understand what he was saying. "It was best for her to be on the farm anyway. 'This city is no place to raise a child, Jacob,' she said to me."

"No, of course it isn't," she said automatically, as she tried to mentally fit him somehow into the story of her misplaced life.

"Oh, but here I go, forgetting myself again." He chuckled as he released her hand and patted the pockets of his jacket as if he were looking for something. "I promised your mother I'd give you her letter the very first thing when you arrived! You look just like her, you know."

"My ... mother?" She echoed his words, placing her fingers to her mouth to cover the shocked reaction.

He heard the tone of her voice and looked at her pale face in dismay. Removing his searching hand from an inside pocket, he pulled out the nearest chair and motioned for her to sit. Candyce looked with alarm at her stricken friend, and then over her shoulder to make sure Marcus was nearby in the event they had to make a quick exit.

"I apologize." His words were very heartfelt. "You must be very tired after your journey here. I know your family is from foreign parts and it is a long and arduous journey to New Orleans."

"Longer than you think," she whispered to him as he finally retrieved the paper he was looking for.

Jasmine gently took the parchment he offered and held it closely to her chest. She didn't have to open it to know what it was, but the final proof that the letter was truly meant for her made it carry all the meaning she hoped for when she first began her quest for answers.

She unfolded the crisp white paper, quite the contrast to the yellowed version she had initially held so dear, and ran her fingers over the words there.

My dearest Jasmine, it began ... But by now, she knew the words by heart.

"Is my mother here?" She asked the first question that popped into her mind. Really, it was the only question there could be for her right then.

"I'm sorry, I thought you knew." His face fell and she was instantly afraid he was going to tell her that her mother was dead. He carefully pulled the chair opposite of Jasmine out from under the table and motioned for Candyce to sit. When she shook her head, obviously choosing to remain at Jasmine's side, he took the seat himself.

"She had the sickness, she told me, when she first came here," he explained. "She said she had done everything she could for the King, and now she was doing what she could for her daughter. She knew you were coming when she hired me on to be the guardian of the estate, but she didn't know when."

"What was wrong with her?" Jasmine sat straight up in the chair, trying to learn everything she could about her mother. "Did she tell you that?"

"Well, whatever she had, the doctors here couldn't help her. She took her ease until she was well enough to travel back. She said she was returning home where they could treat her. I never asked her exactly where that was. I figured if she wanted me to know, she'd have told me."

"So, she's not ... " Jasmine couldn't bring herself to say the words that she feared the most, and so her silence finished the thought.

"Dead?" He looked surprised, and then smiled widely. "Heaven's no! Not when she left here, anyway. In fact ... "

His voice dwindled off in the distance but Jasmine didn't hear it. She felt like she could jump out of her skin, like there were a million things she needed to do to find the woman from her dreams. She was so distracted by the revelation that she was unaware he had asked her the same question three times in a row before Candyce tugged at her sleeve.

"I'm so sorry." She cast around for an excuse, realizing then that he had been speaking the entire time. "I guess I am very tired from my journey, after all. What were you saying?"

"If you can just appoint a new guardian and give me your information for the deed, I can be on my way to the farm," he tapped his pen on the large, familiar looking envelope lying on the table in front of her.

"No way," she whispered, picking it up and sliding the property document out carefully. It was eerie to see it brand new, even if her name wasn't on it yet.

He didn't bat an eye when she numbly gave him her address in California and he wrote it down in his ledger.

"Now, for the guardian of the estate?" He looked to Jasmine, who in turn set her gaze on Candyce. Even if she had a dozen people to choose from, she knew who she wanted it to be.

"What do I have to do?" The petite woman asked nervously as Jasmine pulled her outside to try to convince her to take the job. Marcus perked up as they exited, but turned his attention back to the doorway when it became obvious they were just stepping out.

"He said all you have to do is watch the library and make sure nothing is removed and no one suspicious enters the building."

"How do I know who is suspicious?" She sounded very distressed, but Jasmine saw that sparkle in her eyes and knew the woman could handle most anything.

"The pay is better than the work you're doing now and I'll bet it's a lot safer, too. Besides, he said you could hire a few folks to help you run the estate." She nodded in the direction of Marcus and his sister. "I think I know two good people to help you out."

It didn't take long for Candyce to realize this prospect was much better than her current living arrangements, but the knowledge that she could help her friends swayed her most, Jasmine thought, and she admired that.

Once everyone came back inside, Marcus and Marie included, Jacob showed them the upstairs flat where they would reside during their stay. Jasmine was quite surprised herself to learn that there were accommodations overhead, but she should have guessed as much from the balcony above.

Most of the rooms upstairs had been closed off when the single caretaker had stayed behind after his family traveled to the country, but it didn't take long to open them again. Marcus motioned for her to come out in the hall, which she willingly did as the other two women explored their rooms with delight.

"Thank you for such a chance." He smiled at her with so much loyalty that her heart just melted at the sincerity of it. She noticed again that his manner of speaking was much clearer outside of the bordello. "My sister and I will do everything we can to protect them books and keep you safe here. If I go quick, I can have all our things back before Miss Lulu stirs. I'm sure Marie will be more'n happy to stay with the shop and give it a good blessin' if you and Miss Candyce are still going to market?"

"Yes, we do have to go to the market." The magnitude of everything that happened had nearly sidetracked her, but somehow all her discoveries seemed hollow without the thought of Hayden at her side. It felt like he should have been right there when she discovered the book shop. Perhaps she was finding her path to the future instead of the answers to her past. Still, she was curious about one thing Marcus had said.

"What do you mean, she can give the shop a blessing?" As she asked he gave her a strange look; she realized it must be one of those "what is a president?" sort of questions.

"You know, miss." He laughed with ease, though he humored her with an answer anyway. "Cleanse the house of bad spirits and ward it against 'em ever crossing the doorstep. She's the best this city has."

She almost disregarded his offer, but then Jasmine briefly remembered the evening before. She had fallen asleep with the thought in her mind that anything is possible and just because she didn't understand it, didn't mean it couldn't happen.

"Set it up, Marcus. Let's get some blessings going on in this house."

"There you are," Jacob's voice carried down the hallway. Marie was just opening the heavy drapes in the living quarters and the lavishly decorated hall began to reveal itself in the new light. He had the large envelop in his hand and he was beaming. It looked like he had donned a traveling coat in the meantime, and she was sure he must be anxious to get back to his wife and at least one child she knew of.

He held out the paper for her approval, and as she took it she could see that it was filled out exactly the way she remembered.

"If everything looks in order, I'll seal this envelope and deliver it to my firm. They will send it to your California address when the process is complete." He took the thick parchment from her nerveless fingers and almost sealed it right there before she grabbed it from his hand.

"Wait!" Her voice almost cracked with panic as she hastily opened the flap again.

"I'm sorry." He truly looked apologetic. "Is there another address you wish to have this posted to?"

"The location is fine, Jacob. It's more like a matter of when I need it sent," she said quietly as she tucked the letter from her mother, along with the key that had stayed with her so faithfully, inside with the other paperwork.

"Oh, you don't have to do that," he said as the heavy brass object went in. "I have other copies. I have already given one to Candyce and Miss Marie."

"No, Jacob," she gave him a reassuring look. "It has to be this one."

"Anything you like." He seemed very cheery, and she knew his suitcase was probably sitting outside the door. "When did you want this to arrive?"

Leaning toward him so that she might whisper in his ear, Jasmine gave him the exact date she remembered receiving it in the year 2008. If Marcus overheard the future delivery plans his blank expression didn't reveal any skepticism. Jasmine didn't notice the dubious look on the old caretaker's face, but it soon turned to a steadfast mask of loyalty when she asked that he verbally give her his word on the matter. There was no doubt he would do as she asked anyway, but she couldn't afford to explain to anyone how she knew that.

♦

The sun was much higher in the sky when they came near the market, and it was very crowded this late in the day. Candyce was in high spirits and her mood was wearing off on Jasmine despite her nervous excitement.

She knew why she was so worried about seeing this artist. So much depended on him being the person she so desperately needed him to be. If he was truly the man she met her first night in New Orleans, there was no doubt he could help her get back to Hayden. If he wasn't, no harm would be done to him, and she would be sent on her way without any answers.

If there was one place the city must be different from her time, she thought, it had to be at the market. And mostly because she was quite sure there weren't cages of live chickens and bales of cotton, alongside racks of dried frogs and freshly slaughtered hogs there, a century later. One thing was sure ... it could never smell as bad as it did right now.

"Part of what you smell is the river, you know." Candyce looked over at her wrinkled nose with sympathy, patting her arm.

The market was set up along a street, and crowds of people milled around on the pavement as they browsed the stands. She was distracted by a set of cauldrons on a nearby lot with some sort of bubbling brew inside. There were hand-printed signs next to the cast iron giants, but they were written in some kind of Creole/French dialect she couldn't understand. Whatever was in there, and she wasn't sure she wanted to know, people lined up around the block to hand over some coins and receive a bottle of the liquid. It must have been special, because they all walked away like they had gold in their grasp.

"That's Miss Hattie's cure for the malaria," Candyce filled her in when she noticed Jasmine's attention was drawn that way. "She lived in the swamp so long she must know the remedy if she's still breathin.' It hasn't been too many years gone since the outbreak killed damn near everybody in the city, seems like."

Jasmine was fascinated by the look of hope on the faces of the people gathered in front of the display. Many were obviously servants sent by their masters to retrieve the special concoction, but there were plenty of middle class people who weren't ashamed to stand in line to get a taste of Hattie's brew.

The horn of a vintage motor car sounded off directly behind her, and she was startled by how out of place it seemed at the marketplace. The loud, piercing interruption came a second time, and Jasmine pushed her way up onto the sidewalk to make room for the obviously impatient driver.

The nearby buggies with their gently trained horses pulled a little at their tie ups, but otherwise the sea of Sunday shoppers parted for the self important fellow.

"There he is!" Candyce stood on the curb, pointing her finger over the heads of the tide of people who had flowed in the wake of the vehicle.

Jasmine followed her direction, full of excitement, and immediately saw the display of paintings. She was overwhelmed by the assortment of art that showcased her face, her hair and even her figure in the most appealing and flattering nature. But that was nothing compared to her first glimpse of the man who put his hand to the canvas.

It was Lucas for sure, and he was just as handsome and as charming as she remembered that first evening in the city. She saw the sunlight fall on his honey colored hair, the sparkle in his amber tinted eyes as he was courted by a fine lady so boldly on the street. She saw from the distance the paint on his hands as he so shyly hid them away from his paramour ...

Oh my God, it can't be. Her mind reeled from the thought that suddenly lit her mind like a thousand lights on Christmas. As she stood there, looking at the artist among his many followers, she saw the boy he used to be; the child who had gazed on her with open adoration at the Monastery of Darkenbane. It was Hayden's young cousin, Luke.

She wanted to run through the crowd, screaming his name. The street was thick with people but she began to push through on impulse, not caring who she might displace among the throng of shoppers who stood between her and her chance to find Hayden. Some resisted, but most moved to the side when they decided this strangely dressed woman was obviously crazy and not worth a struggle.

She came nearly within earshot, and considered shouting his name because she couldn't wait to breach the distance. Before she could make a sound, however, the insistent motorcar that had paraded through the crowd just a moment before slid along the curb and stopped directly in front of Lucas. A white gloved chauffer emerged from the driver side, and stepped smartly along to the back door.

A man in a black suit exited the vehicle, though she could see very little of him with his back to her. The people standing by seemed fascinated by his car, and they crowded near him to get a better look at the owner. He tensed up as they came within physical contact and turned back on the mass with a frown.

It was her first glimpse of his face, but it was the only one she needed to see. The scowl Ference gave to the onlookers turned away most except the very hardy of souls, and he shivered with displeasure at the few who remained close.

"Lucas!" she did cry out then, but only to warn him. No one heard her over the hawkers and buyers, least of all the artist who frowned at the newcomer. Jasmine silently prayed he remembered who the terrible man was, and her prayers were answered as Lucas visibly bristled when he came near. Ference uttered what appeared to be a few distant, stern words to the young artist and he immediately held his head in defeat.

She couldn't believe what she was seeing. She wanted to run through the gathering of curious spectators, but with a city like New Orleans, a heavy crowd could coalescence in an instant if there was a chance to witness drama. The handsome young man raised his head and nodded in compliance at the villain before him. With a slow and regretful gesture, he reached forth his arm and shook the hand of Ference. Jasmine was stunned by the display and turned away with the sudden feeling she should not be seen by either of the two men. She spun around and forced her way back through the dispersing crowd.

"Wait," Candyce called out after her friend, reversing her direction while she attempted to dart through the opening left by Jasmine's passage.

She couldn't hear her. All she could her was her heart thundering through her veins with anger and dismay. The beautiful city around her, everything she might have appreciated or taken joy from, seemed grey and lifeless with the thought Lucas had betrayed her.

"What's wrong?" Candyce asked with concern when she caught up to her friend. "I thought you wanted to see him more than anything in the world?"

"I thought I did, too," she answered, and her tone let Candyce know that she didn't want to talk about it for the time being. She was afraid the devastation would show in her voice and she wasn't willing to let go of her hope just yet. She felt if she could just have some time alone to think, she might figure out a way to return to Darkenbane on her own. A piece seemed to be missing, and if this clown car of a ride could just slow down for a minute, she could think of it.

Her friend appeared to understand that all too well, and so she walked alongside the dark haired beauty in silence; it was exactly was Jasmine needed just then.

The disappointment from her nearly disastrous encounter with

Lucas weighed heavily on her conscience, but it couldn't completely dampen the growing feeling of excitement that began to build as they returned to the shop where she knew her mother had lived. There could be a million clues, and she intended to look for each one of them ... Just as soon as she figured out what the red paint was in the door frame of the book store.

"Marcus?" she called out in a polite, but horrified, voice. "Is this blood in the doorway?"

"Well, it has to be," he answered her honestly, but she could tell by the look on his face he knew she wasn't overly familiar with Marie's ways.

He put a comforting arm around her shoulders, like he might do for a little sister.

"If it makes you feel any better, we havin' that chicken for dinner."

"You have no idea how many ways that makes me not feel better," she remarked as she forced herself to enter the first room, stepping over the threshold in an exaggerated manner.

"You said let's get some blessings up in here," he reminded her reproachfully, and she had to agree with his statement.

Candyce excused herself with a knowing grin. She vaguely let them know she was off to help Marie with the cooking, but she was more likely hiding the evidence.

Marie must have gone around the shop earlier and lit some of the gas lights in the reading room while they were gone, though it was still afternoon and the sunlight came in through the large windows at the front of the building. For the first time she noticed the painting on the wall between two of the fixtures, but she must have glanced over it a time or two before she was aware. It hung exactly where she remembered, and though she had intended to mention the place to Marcus, he unknowingly fulfilled the destiny of the picture on his own.

For a very brief moment, she almost felt like she had no control over her future. Things like the painting and the letter from her mother made it seem obvious it had already been written no matter what she did. With great determination and a view no one could ever say was not progressive, Jasmine finally decided someone had to write history, so it may as well be her since she was knee-deep in it already.

Still, her eyes lingered on the portrait and it was difficult to suppress the deep feeling of sadness over her discovery at the market that morning. Marcus seemed to sense that she needed some time alone and asked her permission join the two women in the kitchen.

Her mind was filled with so many overwhelming thoughts that she wandered around the sitting room aimlessly, consciously avoiding any visual contact with the painting until she sorted through her conflicting emotions. Finally pacing the length of the room and back, Jasmine found herself standing at the same table where she had originally found the old book—the one she regretfully left in Lucas' hands.

The reading candle was nearly burned down as far as she remembered and with no one around to witness her magic, she took the book of matches from her bag.

"Abracadabra." She smirked, but quickly lit the wick before the paper match could burn her fingers. She wasn't sure what she was going to do tomorrow, but she was determined to write an entry in her book about Lucas now, before she could forget any of the details.

The feeble pen eked out her knowledge and she cursed herself under her breath for forgetting to ask one of her new friends for a better one. A quill and bottle might have done the job more admirably than this disposable model. Still, just writing down the scene helped her focus on the matter at hand, and she felt like she was accomplishing something.

The sounds of laughter upstairs buoyed her spirits, as well as the smell of Cajun food drifting down off the stove. The rich and spicy aroma was so distracting, in fact, that she hadn't noticed the ambient sound emanating from outside the room.

It was a gentle cascade, the relaxing trickle of falling water that finished in a symphony of delicate splashes, and she wondered how she hadn't heard it before. Perhaps Jacob kept it turned off with his family so far away and Marie activated the device again when she opened the house.

It was the fountain, of course.

How could I have been here so long and never looked at the fountain? She immediately closed the book with all of its secrets. Laying it gently on the small table, she stood and proceeded to walk through the small library.

The hardwood floor was pristine and she could smell the oil soap that coated the recently polished surface. The books lined the shelves in the same way she remembered, but they told her much more now. If her mother truly brought them here, these volumes might contain the secrets of Hayden's people, her people maybe, for that matter. If only she could get back, she could tell him about the treasure inside that room.

She had purposefully left the door to the parlor open, and the glow from the reading lights cast enough illumination for her to see across the distance to the courtyard exit. She didn't stride boldly across the library floor as she might have done in the past; carefully and quietly, Jasmine crept across the glossy floorboards. The door opened without a sound on the other side and she entered the courtyard slowly, pulling it closed behind her. It was late afternoon by then, probably early evening, but the sun had gone down behind the roof of the adjacent building and it left her in a long, cool shadow. She saw the angels first, their hands still covering their faces, but the tears hadn't yet eroded the marble of their skin.

The fountain stood at the center, and it was every bit as beautiful and perfect as she remembered the night that Hayden came through. Jasmine rushed to the edge like all the answers she might ever need had been gathered inside and were awaiting her discovery, but all she saw was a rippling pattern of warm, hazy water.

She tried hard to be disappointed, but the real truth was that she stood at the place where she first met her love, and the memory of it filled her heart.

She slowly sat on the edge of the lower tier and pulled her purse onto her lap. With a quick look around to make sure she was completely alone, she opened the bag and freed the silver ring that Hayden had given her on the night he began his strange courtship. The water tumbled with a trickling cadence over the rim of each level and she felt the pull of the rhythm. Lulled by the soothing flow, she was almost unaware of her actions as she held the ring in the center of her palm, absently stroking the rim with her fingertips.

Her head was filled with the vivid memory of their first night at the cabin in the mountains, of the first time he held her close when she sat on his lap in the yellow leaves and how he kissed her with unbridled passion next to the ruined stones where another fountain had been ages ago ...

The ring grew instantly warm, and a sharp vibration emanated through the skin of her palm, jarring the bones in her hand. She reacted before her mind could rationalize the occurrence and her tingling fingers promptly dropped the silver object into the fountain.

She jumped to her feet in dismay, leaning over the edge to see where it had fallen so she could retrieve it. At first Jasmine thought the rippling water was playing tricks on her eyes, but as she scanned the bottom of the basin she couldn't deny that the ring was quickly growing larger beneath the surface.

As it expanded in size, it began to rise to the top. Everything inside her wanted to reach in the water and grab it before anything else could happen, but she was fascinated by the transformation. She thought it would have to stop when it came up against the center tiers of marble, but the ring passed through as if they didn't exist. Finally it came to rest in a perfect circle against the outer rim of the fountain.

Jasmine stood stock still for a minute, and when nothing happened she looked cautiously into the pool. All she could see were leaves and a bit of sky reflected along the bottom. She glanced over her shoulder to the door of the library and thought of her new friends upstairs, just making dinner. She also thought of Hayden, and the way he kneeled before her on the flagstones of the garden that night when her heart promised to be his.

Jasmine slung the travel bag securely over her shoulder. She didn't even have time to tell them she was going. There really was no decision to make, after all.

♦

The light tapping on the glass of the front door went on for quite a while before Candyce heard it and came downstairs. At first she thought Jasmine was moving things around in the parlor, and was surprised to see that the front room was empty and the door to the darkened library was ajar. After a quick look by the fountain, she realized the entire downstairs was abandoned and the sound was actually a gentle knock outside.

"I saw the lights on in the reading room for the first time in ages," the handsome young man explained as soon as she opened the door. “I hope you don’t mind that I’ve stopped by to introduce myself.”

Despite her friend’s baffling reaction to him at the market earlier that day, Candyce was more than awed by the presence of the charming artist at the front step. After all, she had been an admirer of his work for quite a while and Jasmine hadn’t given her any explanation for her behavior that afternoon.

“If you would like to come inside, I can call for the lady of the house,” she said as properly as she could, and drifted back a few feet for Lucas to enter. He came forward like he intended to accept her offer, but came up short as he reached the threshold. He glanced down with an almost imperceptible look of frustration, but it was fleeting and Candyce was sure she must have mistaken it.

“I can’t imagine where she would be,” the woman said in an effort to keep him engaged. “It was not but a moment ago that she sat right here, but she seems to have disappeared into thin air.”

For just an instant his handsome face fell with heart wrenching disappointment and he seemed utterly defeated. She desperately tried to think of something to say, compelled to reassure him, but before she could speak another word he lifted his head and gave her a stunningly beautiful smile.

“I am quite sure that you would be a wonderful companion in her stead.” His voice was sweet and charming. “I have the shop just across the square and I would be honored if you could join me tonight in the courtyard for a glass of wine. We might talk about the wonderful lady of the house and you can tell me of the adventures you two have had together.”

Candyce nodded, completely under his spell as she stepped through the door. He held his hand out to her as if she was a lady of the highest importance and she allowed him to lead her away.

As Marcus and Marie stood frowning on the balcony above, the faithful musician had one thought on his mind though he didn’t understand why it would worry him so much above all else. He just wished to Heaven that he had never told Candyce about that envelope and the strange date it was to arrive in California.

Chapter Ten

Jasmine hadn't consciously meant to, but before she touched the ring her shoulders had tensed and she braced her legs like maybe it would steady her figure so she could be ready on the other side. She still wasn't sure how a split second could feel like forever, and she also couldn't stop herself from holding her breath, but if her knees hadn't been locked up when she came through the other side she wouldn't have fallen like a board, straight over that chunk of rock at her toes.

Thankfully, the ground beneath her cheek was warm and wet. Very slowly she set her palms on the saturated surface and pushed herself up into a kneeling position. No one was in sight, and she wasn't sure if she was relieved that nobody witnessed her plunge, or concerned she was alone in a forest.

The leaves on the surrounding trees were bright green, and sweet blossoms hung from the branches around the clearing. There was a fountain to her right, and she soon discovered it was coated in a slick layer of moss when she reached out a hand to pull her wet knees out of the mud.

Pieces of the stone had crumbled over time, but it was still standing for the most part. She noticed a lengthy crack along the bottom and the numerous decaying leaves that lurked beneath the surface. It didn't take more than a minute for her to figure out that with the fountain in such disrepair there probably wasn't anyone around for miles. It also didn't take long for her to realize this place felt very familiar ...

A light breeze was beginning to stir the hair from her shoulders, and it was cold without a doubt. She shivered a little and a cascade of pink and white petals came down from the surrounding branches with the next gust, swirling around her like a tentative caress as a few daring pieces of the natural garland landed in her hair. The scene was enchanting, Jasmine tried to tell her herself, or it should have been. Something about the cutting chill and the grey sky over head made her wary in the springtime clearing. And while the tiny petals were not formidable on their own, their accumulation stuck to her skin and began to get in places she didn't think were necessary.

She searched for the path and the moment she stepped foot on it a vision of Hayden's face popped into her head. Her heart stopped beating for a moment when she realized that she had nearly left the clearing without retrieving the silver ring.

The friendly breeze that kissed her hair a moment before was rapidly becoming an invasive gale. The fragile petals flew with the current and coated the wet ground like a light layer of snow. It was an eerie scene to say the least, but had she not dropped to her hands and knees next to the fountain when she did, she never would have found the ring under the new sprinkling of silk blossoms.

She stood quickly and tried to find the way once again. It was impossible to detect from the floor of the forest now, but the trees still offered a narrow corridor of passage, much more narrow than she had remembered a moment before.

She went along as quickly as she could with the wet conditions at her feet. Surely her mind was playing tricks on her; the path couldn't be closing up ahead before her very eyes. That was just silly!

Jasmine took a moment to remember where she was. All bets were off on the other side of the fountain and you couldn't spend a lot of time assuming things. If you did, you wouldn't last long. With that thought in mind, she sprinted through the closing branches that seemed to be reaching for her as she passed by. Her beautiful white blouse became snagged and torn, though the leather portions of her traveling gear held up to the snapping twigs and grazing thorns.

She burst from the clearing with a sigh of relief, immediately spinning around to witness the path as it closed in behind her. She really wasn't surprised when it all looked completely still and normal.

I don't even know what normal is anymore, she thought to

herself as she turned away from the forest.

Jasmine thought from that minute forward, nothing that happened to her could mean as much as this very moment. She couldn't imagine anything in this world, or the next for that matter, that could take away the feeling of exultation that swept through her entire being when she saw the mountainside cabin in the distance.

The ancient oak spread its branches over the small wooden structure, just as she remembered. Jasmine stood still, almost afraid that if she moved the whole vision would disappear. She saw that the planks were grey and a little warped, but not nearly as bad as it was when she first encountered it. The front porch was even intact and something that looked like a bench swing drifted back and forth on rusty hinges.

From her distant vantage point she could see the darkened windows set in the old wood. She began to walk toward the cabin when a light flared inside, followed by a wisp of smoke from the crooked chimney on top of the sagging roof.

She immediately froze in place, her heart screaming for her to run forward, that Hayden would be waiting for her inside, but her mind insisted that she should take care in this situation. Deciding to appease both factions, she moved ahead at a slow and steady pace with a watchful eye on the front door. As she grew closer to the building, she noticed freshly cut wood had been stacked on the porch. And although the structure was by no means new, it was certainly in better repair than the first time they had come across it. Of course, there was no telling when that was, she thought to herself.

Her heart beat fast in her chest, but after her disappointment at the book shop when she met Jacob she steeled herself against the disappointment that she would face if her handsome companion was not there. The cold wind had followed her out of the woods and she shivered in the tattered white blouse, wrapping her arms around her shoulders. It played with her like a game of tag as it blew by from many different directions. The last pass it took was particularly bitter, but it carried more than the cold on this sweep. She heard a deep, sorrowful cry coming from the cabin; it was exactly the same way she experienced it before.

Well, she wasn't having any of it this time. The windows were bright and welcoming, for sure. The curling smoke even beckoned to her with promises of a warm fire but she knew better now. It was the same trick as before, except she wasn't going to fall for it this time around.

With long strides that were almost angry, she covered the distance to the cabin in just a few seconds. The floorboards on the porch barely registered her weight as she leaped up, completely skipping the steps.

It was amazing how real the wood burning fire smelled, she thought to herself as she reached for the door. The latch was firmly closed and not a hint of rust covered the handle. The desperately sad cry still came from the interior, but she knew it would all stop when she opened the door and stepped inside to view the cold, vacant room. With no further hesitation, she popped the latch and swung the door inward.

The first thing she noticed was the wave of dry heat that hit her in the face. She was startled when the wind took the door from her nerveless grasp and banged it up against the wall inside.

She covered her mouth, eyes wide with surprise as the figure of a man sprung from the ground in front of the fireplace. She began to rush forward at once, when she realized it wasn't Hayden.

He had his sword in his hand before she could blink, and as he turned his tear-stained face in her direction, a look of confused recognition entered his crazed eyes. It was only an instant of hesitation, but that was all it took for her to realize she knew who this person was.

He looked very different in a suit of leather traveling clothes, but she was sure the man who stood before her was Malcolm of Ravenswood, Captain of the Guard.

Chapter Eleven

"Lady Jasmine?" he said a little roughly, his eyes clearing as he looked down at the tip of his sword, poised and ready to run her through.

She nodded at him, afraid her voice might fail her at the moment. He immediately dropped the offending blade with disgust and she noticed his hands were trembling.

"Why are you here? Where is my Lord Amarynn?" He looked past her and through the door as if he expected Hayden to come through at any moment.

"He isn't here, Malcolm." She stretched a hand forward to comfort him, reaching for his shoulder. She desperately wished Hayden would come walking through that doorway to help her, and at the same time her heart twisted painfully with the knowledge of everything the Captain had gone through. She didn't know what she would do if something so terrible would happened to her, but she was more than aware of the mistake he was about to make.

"You have to leave here at once, my Lady." He lifted his head once more and she could see that he was thinking clearly now. "It isn't safe for you here."

"It isn't safe for you here, either," she responded, and was astonished when he grabbed her up as lightly as a feather and took her onto the front porch.

"Put me down. I have to talk to you." She squirmed in his arms, and with reluctance, he set her feet gently onto the wooden planks.

"I have many regrets, Lady Jasmine," he growled in a low tone and she could see the new determination in his eyes. "One of them will not be you."

"That's what I want to tell you." She stood straight and tall, trying to look him in the eye and match his will. "I know what you're going to do. If you choose this course, you will die."

He met her stare with the most honest, sincere look of torment she could ever imagine on the face of another human being.

"I hope so."

Jasmine found that no words seemed an adequate argument next to the tragedy he had experienced, and her defiant stance quickly faded to one of sorrow.

"It has already begun." He took her hand gently, and even in his darkest moment he held her with compassion. "I have placed my confession and worked the rift open. It won't be long now until the tear spreads and I have to take my chances. It would have cost Lord Amarynn dearly to give me the small amount of information that he did, and I will not let my folly cost him his greatest love as well."

With a kind and gentle pull, he led her off the porch and into the grass. She found she didn't have the heart to dispute his wishes and wondered if she even should.

"Am I his greatest love?" she asked solemnly with a whisper, and for the first time the shadow of a smile crossed his haggard face.

"Do you not see the way he looks at you, my Lady?"

She had indeed, but she had spent her whole life dreaming of a love that never seemed to appear, of a handsome young man next to a fountain that could never exist. When Hayden came into her life, it felt like her heart had been dormant all those years and at his touch she knew a whole world of existence that she could never have imagined before. The only problem was, she didn't know if any of it was real. And if it wasn't, she didn't know how she might go on after knowing the way it could be.

"Let me tell you about love." Malcolm smiled then, and his eyes glazed over with a far off memory.

"My life was amazing. I was the youngest Captain of the Guard ever to be seen in the Amarynn rule and my wife had given me two beautiful daughters. I tell you—" He stopped for a moment with a tender laugh. "I thought the sun rose and set on the three women in my life, they were so lovely. The youngest was but a child when the war began, though we knew she would be the greatest beauty of them all with her natural blonde hair and blue eyes."

He stopped them, and passed his hand over his eyes as if to clear the visions he held there.

"We lost her during the second year of the war. They never recovered her body and not knowing how she died was more painful than knowing she had passed at all. There was so much confusion then; the entire court was making ready to move to the monastery and many of the citizens had fallen sick from the shift sickness. I never blamed them for not finding her, but I always regretted that she would have no grave for me to carve our family crest upon."

They stood out on the spring time grass and it occurred to Jasmine that if she could keep him talking, perhaps he wouldn't go inside and become lost in the void forever.

"I'm sure you did what you had to do." She looked for any kind of comforting words, but she thought he didn't appear to notice what she was saying until he turned to look at her again.

"It was my fault they died. I was so full of fear after we lost Jessica that I broke the rules and sent them to safety when I was charged with my duty to guard the crossroads." He sighed. "I knew the war could shatter the dimensions of existence in Ravenswood, but it was not until Prince Amarynn told me my men and I had been isolated all this while that I truly knew my family could be in danger. I never told another soul that I sent them away, you see."

Jasmine nodded, realizing the horror of it all. She had no doubt he intended to slip off and see them at the earliest opportunity. He never got that chance, because time passed differently at the crossroads. Malcolm of Ravenswood didn't know it then, but he had all the time in the world; unfortunately, his family hadn't.

No wonder Darkenbane enforced such strict rules about interfering with the timelines, she realized, deep in thought over the complicated web of time that seemed to bind everyone. You can't unravel one thread and go on. Eventually the entire weave will come undone when the balance is altered and the other strands move and strain to support the whole.

While she considered the implications of all the damage that had been done, Malcolm reached into a pouch that was tied securely to the inside of his jerkin. He produced a large, golden signet ring and with hopeful fingers he held it out to her.

She took it and saw an exquisite crest carved into the onyx

stone of the oval.

"What is this?" she asked, marveling at the craftsmanship of the object. It must have been a family heirloom passed down for generations and she thought with great sadness that he had no one else to give it to now.

"If you happen across my daughter's grave, will you see to it that our crest is put onto the stone?" He smiled raggedly and she knew that it was his last act of salvation.

"Of course I will," she agreed, thinking silently to herself that she would turn over every rock between the castle and the monastery to find her final resting place if it was the last thing she ever did.

He took her hand in his and covered the signet with a sure and steady grasp, reminding her overwhelmingly of the night Hayden had given her his own legacy. She saw that he didn't tremble any more and thought that perhaps he had finally made peace with himself.

With no sign of regret, he turned away from her and walked back toward the cabin. When his boot touched the first step of the weathered wood a light came on inside and he smiled to himself, looking back over his shoulder to Jasmine.

"Perhaps I will find my darling Jesi inside as well." His voice was filled with hope as he touched the door.

"Jesi," she repeated vaguely, turning the signet over in her hands as she tried desperately to keep her emotions in check.

The instant the words crossed her lips the blood in her veins turned to ice and she immediately thought back to the girl that Cordelia sent to her quarters that first night at the monastery.

"Jesi!" she called out in realization, but by then, Malcolm didn't hear her. She barely heard herself, because the moment he pushed the door open a thousand sounds seemed to happen at once. At first she thought the ground had shifted beneath her feet but she realized that the grass was growing and dying in ripples right before her eyes. It was like everything that had happened here in the past was happening now, but all at the same instant.

With the effects of the ripple now apparent, she knew she had no time to waste, but instead of running away from the clearing, she darted forward and grabbed Malcolm by his leather belt. With a strong tug she got him back off the porch and onto the bizarre waves of brown and green grass.

"What are you doing!" he shouted with frustration and they struggled on the ground for a moment. He actually got to his feet for a moment, before she grabbed his ankles and he fell headlong just short of the cabin steps. She held on for as long as she could, her muscles weakening against the pull of her frantic companion.

Jasmine's fingers began loosening their hold without her permission, though she tried until the very end. She didn't know if it was long enough, but as he finally escaped her grasp she took comfort in the silence that suddenly surrounded them and she laid her head on her hands in defeat.

At first it was a welcome relief after the cacophony of noise that seemed to drown out the world, but she soon realized there was a big difference between quiet and the complete absence of sound.

Her ears rang in the eerie stillness, and she climbed to her hands and knees in order to check things out.

The sunlight felt weak as it fell onto her aching shoulders and as she looked up into the sky she couldn't see the source. In fact, everything looked a little bit dull and lifeless. That was when she noticed there was no wind. No birds singing, no leaves falling. The landscape appeared almost two dimensional in its cardboard cutout construction.

Malcolm, however, appeared to be very real; and it wouldn't be a stretch at all to say he looked to be more than a little displeased.

"I really have a good reason for all of this," she began a little tentatively, hoping against hope that she actually did.

"Regardless of what you have done, Lady Jasmine, I can't be angry for anything that might happen to me. But I will have to answer to Prince Amarynn if anything happens to you."

"Only if we're really lucky," she muttered under her breath as she stood to her feet and readied her excuse.

"Let me tell you about my serving girl," she smiled as the look on his face turned incredulous. She had to give him some credit though, because he obviously intended to hear what she had to say.

•

"Is it possible? Can this girl at the monastery really be my daughter?" His face was completely transformed by Jasmine's news, and she saw him again for what he once was: handsome, confident and the loyal Captain of the Guard.

"Nothing's impossible," she practically choked on the words. "Believe me, I know."

"If this is the case, I owe you a debt of gratitude I could never repay." He instantly stood and came close to her, his manner excited and earnest.

"Well, it's no biggie." She casually tried to ease his conscience, but jumped back in alarm as he dropped to one knee on the pale ground before her. She was instantly reminded of Hayden, but unlike her Prince, Malcolm didn't take her hand. Instead, he crossed his arms over his knee and lowered his head in reverence.

"Hey, now," she said a little nervously as she reached out her right hand and patted him like she might a puppy she wasn't sure of. "Thanks and all that, but it's not really necessary with me."

"I fear that none of this will matter, my Lady," he spoke with regret as he stood, looking at their surroundings. "While you prevented me from going into the heart of the rift, we were both still caught on the border. If my battle studies serve me well, we're at the outer edge of our dimension, just one moment behind the present."

"No kidding," she exclaimed, joining him in his appraisal. "I think I saw that in a movie once."

"What did they do to rectify their situation in this movie?" He said the last word like it was foreign to him.

"You mean the ones that didn't get eaten? You don't want to know ..." She looked at the tree above the cabin for any sign of life. "Anyway, can't we just use a ring or something to get back? I keep asking if that isn't what you people do."

"A ring creates a doorway between dimensions, from one to the other. It negates the void in between," he instructed her patiently. "And I suspect we're in between."

"Okay," she finally said with a little more understanding. "There has to be something we can try because I have a dinner date and I don't intend to miss it. You'll just have to sit here and think of it, even if it takes forever."

"We have forever, let me assure you," he said evenly. "But I already know there is only one way out of here and the chances of him ever helping me would be infinitesimal."

"Alright, what are we up against?" she asked immediately, ready to do whatever it took to get them back.

"He uses magic, not technology, to travel the realms. To him, time is only something that binds us mortals. Our methods are of little use to him in ways that we can't even understand, though he seems to enjoy playing with pieces of our lives."

As he told her this, a small look of distracted confusion crossed his face as his gaze fell past her and to the woods. Jasmine, however, had a very different reaction to his words as her intuition screamed out with warning. The hairs on the back of her neck stood on end and she shivered in dread. It wasn't a cold breeze at her back. She knew there couldn't be one. It wasn't even the wondrous look of shock on Malcolm's face as he stood instantly frozen in time, his hand still reaching for his sword.

"I am not your enemy, Jasmine." A deep, masculine voice came suddenly from behind, and despite the chill that crept up her spine his breath was hot on her neck.

She tried to turn about quickly but her movements were slow and tedious. She knew right away she wouldn't be able to run; damn, even if she could, where would she go?

His long, blonde hair clung to his naked shoulders and his ageless grey eyes glittered from the depths of the mask with something that resembled intrigue.

The God of the Grove radiated a primal sensuality that sparked her deepest passions, though this desire flew right through her heart and all her thoughts were of Hayden.

"Come with me." The mysterious immortal held out his hand.

Chapter Twelve

His words were seductive, almost compelling. She glanced over her shoulder at the Captain and shook her head to clear her mesmerized thoughts.

"I'll go, but I'll go on one condition," she spoke with a determined gesture toward her friend. She wasn't about to lose Hayden's Captain of the Guard after she saved his life. "He comes with me."

The God of the Grove frowned at her ultimatum, but she could see that same spark of interest grow in his eyes.

"I hardly think you're in a position to be making demands, foolish girl."

"Probably not," she conceded. "But here I am all the same, just making away."

"Your spirit is ... charming," he answered her challenge, and she heard a note of pleasure in his voice.

"Take my hand and we shall all be on our way."

She hesitated for a minute, trying to decide if she could trust him not to leave her friend behind. There was no guarantee, she knew, and at the end she decided she simply had to take him at his word.

After all, she thought to herself with a little sarcasm, *in all my worldly experience these immortal god-types always keep a promise.*

She took his hand with resignation and he smiled beneath the half mask that she was coming to recognize him by. She hoped it was a mask, anyway.

As soon as her skin made contact with his fingers, the entire slope of the mountainside flooded with a white mist. She braced herself for the excruciating cold that was sure to follow, but to her surprise, the noninvasive vapors merely crept upward along her figure until her vision was obscured. She could see nothing save the whiteout, and only the connection she had with the stranger's hand let her know she wasn't alone.

Jasmine had been holding her breath when the mist engulfed the upper part of her body, but that only lasted so long before she was forced to gasp for air and take in the strange, white substance. Her eyes squeezed shut and for a moment her lungs felt heavy, but the sensation quickly passed.

When she dared to open them again, she found herself inside a large wooden structure of some type. The scent of cedar permeated the area, as well as the sweet fragrance of new blossoms.

The room was unlike anything she had ever seen before. The walls were solid wood, but the ceiling appeared to be a thick covering of vines and leaves. Vegetation grew from crevices along the gnarled paneling and real fireflies flitted all around them. It felt like a house, but it looked like a garden and it was probably the most beautiful thing she had ever seen.

"Welcome to my home," her host spoke with pleasure at her reaction. She turned in the direction of his voice and saw Malcolm standing near; his face must have mirrored her own with wonder. "If you would care to follow me, you'll want time to prepare for the ball," he said cryptically.

"The ball?" She was really starting to feel like she had to repeat everything that was said in an effort to understand what was going on.

"One time each year I open my realm for all mortals to celebrate the feast of Candlemas. For them, tonight is that night. Are you familiar with the occasion?"

"Please," she nearly scoffed at his question. "I grew up in California with all the Wiccans. Are you kidding?" But as a history professor, she knew that Candlemas was a gentle, ancient Celtic celebration that welcomed spring and closed the door on the dark days of winter. She was amazed it was practiced here in this reality as well as her own.

She followed her host down the corridor, contemplating just how closely their worlds were intertwined, when he stopped in front of the first room and motioned respectfully for Malcolm to enter. Once the captain was inside, he took her further down the passage until they came to another doorway, and this one was entwined with a lovely vine of fully blooming jasmine. She thought it was a nice touch and wondered why he would trouble himself.

Just as he was about to turn away, the strange immortal hesitated and then winked at her from behind the mask.

"Of course, if you need more time to make yourself ready, I can arrange it."

She didn't doubt it; what was time for someone like him? Without an answer, she entered her chamber.

It was a strange mix of nature and man-made influences to say the least. She had a difficult time deciding if the carpet at her feet was a soft, mossy layer of plant growth or some type of synthesized fabric. The bed was designed to resemble a four-post ensemble, but the wood that made up the poles grew right into the ceiling with a natural twist of polished grain. Silk drapes and veils hung all around the room, in a wide selection of indigos and greens.

She might have thought the eclectic gathering of so many blooming plants and flowers in one place would be overwhelming, but it was truly a masterpiece of presentation and the scented blossoms complimented each other perfectly.

There was no fire burning, or even a fireplace in the room for that matter, but a basin-like porcelain bowl sat on a pedestal near the night table and she noticed right away that the water was steaming.

Then she saw the vanity. It looked like something straight out of her dreams, with a mysterious gathering of pots and vials resting on the surface. The large, round mirror was polished to perfection and she was drawn to the delicate items laid out before her.

No matter how much she wished she could avoid her tattered reflection in the mirror, it insisted on presenting itself and she was forced to look it over with dismay. She had to hope that some change of clothing came along with the gift of cosmetics or she would be an unsightly attendant for the night's event.

Just as she began to explore the rest of the area, a quiet knock interrupted her expedition and she casually crossed the room to open the door with no thought as to who might be there. As far as she knew, only Malcolm and their strange host were privy to her whereabouts.

She was stunned the moment she opened the door and saw

who was standing in the corridor.

"My Lady Jasmine," Lucas began in earnest, and her instincts caused her to back away from the opening and his presence there. He instantly took it as a sign to enter and came into the room without hesitation.

"I don't know how you found me, or what you hope to accomplish, but I think you've done enough already." She firmly held up her hand and he frowned at her reaction.

"Finding you has been my single charge for as long as I can remember," he tried to explain again, though she didn't let him get far.

"Alright then, you've found me. Now you can go on your merry little way and stab somebody else in the back."

"Candyce told me about the trip you and she took to the market." He hung his head a little with the admission, losing some of his bravado. "I can only guess what you saw there."

Jasmine's thoughts were swirling with a thousand ways to remove him from her presence when his statement jarred her out of her reverie.

"What did you do with Candyce," she asked, suddenly interested in what he had to say. She silently cursed herself for inadvertently putting the kind woman in harm's way.

"Your friend is quite alright and I will be happy to explain my encounter with her," he assured, holding up his hands. "But first, I must tell you of the reason I allied myself with my Lord Ference."

"My Lord Ference," Jasmine spat in disgust, and the look on his face was grim under her gaze.

"You must understand ... I was there in the royal chambers when you vanished. I witnessed the horrendous thing that Cordelia did to you when I was just a child. She sent me to the Darkenbane monks in an effort to silence me, but she had no idea how adept I could become."

She was shocked into silence by his revelation and immediately thought of the young, gentle boy he had been. She knew then what he had seen must have traumatized him immensely. With no conscious awareness, her face took on a look of compassion and he was encouraged to continue his tale.

"I struggled in avowed silence at the academy and my work far outclassed any initiate in the history of the order. But no matter how adept I became that first year, I could do nothing to trace the portal she used to send you away. I was torn by my innocent infatuation for you and my loyalty to Prince Amarynn who entrusted me with your care. Either way, I failed you both ..."

"Why help Ference, after what that woman did to me?" she whispered, almost afraid of the answer he would give.

"Don't you see?" He spread his hands before her in a plea for understanding. "He needed someone who would break the vows of the order and recruit others within the ranks to serve him. I needed to know where his sister, Cordelia, sent you on that fateful day you vanished through the portal."

A cold wave of realization washed over her and she knew then that Lucas was just a pawn in another man's game; but what a terrible piece he was.

"You had no idea he would become so powerful," she stated out loud, as a dreadful kind of understanding fell over her.

"It was well known in my time that he was displeased with the Amarynn rule, and Hayden's refusal to marry his sister only angered him more. When I agreed to help him in order to discover the start of your trail, I had no idea it would lead to an army; I had no idea it would lead to the very war that destroyed our kingdom when I was just a newborn."

"Oh my God," Jasmine said with total clarity. "Ference is the key. He went back to the place where Hayden was still a child and began to unravel the fabric of his existence."

"I never meant to hurt anyone." His face was filled with sorrow and regret. "I only wanted to save you. I spent so many years in and out of time trying to find you that I almost forgot why. I grew up alone during many different time periods in that crescent city where I knew you would land eventually. All those years gone by for me ... but to you, it was a matter of days."

She didn't know what to say to him as he stood there, his guilt and shame complete as he finally confessed. It wasn't directly his fault, but he was still the person responsible for everything that happened to her, and to her family.

"My whole life was thrown off track because of you," she inadvertently said it out loud, though it was a thought she meant to keep inside.

He stood up tall, then, steeling himself before her. A look of pure determination settled on his face and he bowed stiffly.

"I will go back, and I will do what I can to make things right for you."

His words echoed with eerie familiarity in her ears, but she couldn't quite place them.

"How can you fix what happened? What can you possibly do?" she asked incredulously, and as the question left her lips she felt a strange sensation, a moment of selfish greed, maybe. Did she really want him to make it all go away? Was she sure that she could give Hayden up to a history made right in the end? Her whole life had been spent searching for clues to her identity. Now she found it mattered a lot less than her present feelings for a man who felt like he could be her future.

"I know what pathways Ference used to change the past. I helped him after all." His voice was stronger now and though he still showed signs of a guilty conscience, he was starting to make sense.

"I can take the books he used for research and send them to safety. With the proper amount of study by the Sensors, the lines he crossed could be repaired and our land can be healed! I will go back to a place before it started and I will find someone I can trust to help me move those tomes when the time is right."

He turned before she could say another word and a chill ran up her spine as he strode to the door.

Like someone walked on my grave, the superstitious thought entered her head, but she dismissed the feeling as she ran to follow him.

"Lucas," she called after him in the corridor, thinking of the envelope and the painting in the shop. "You can't go back. It won't change anything."

He stopped in his tracks and turned to face her. She thought he would be angry at her statement, but instead he gave her a comforting smile as he spoke his parting words.

"I have a feeling I'll see you again, though you may not know who I am."

"Is it always that way?" she asked him softly, but a moment later he was gone.

♦

Jasmine knew she should be angry with Lucas for everything

that had transpired, but as she entered her chamber once more she found she didn't have it in her heart. She even went as far as to hope he survived his quest.

It must have grown dark outside during their interlude, because the interior of her room was far dimmer than she remembered a moment ago. Softly glowing rocks that she never noticed in the daytime began to radiate a diffused type of light all around the base of the walls.

Somehow her encounter with Lucas had buoyed her spirits. Maybe it was that she knew he hadn't intentionally betrayed her, or the idea they had both been through so much together. Either way, she found herself feeling hopeful and ready to prepare for the celebration that evening. After all, it wasn't like she got invited to a ball on Candlemas every day, and every minute she spent here was another minute she could find a way to get back to Hayden.

She didn't know how she missed it before, but hanging amidst the veils and draperies throughout her room was a dress. Well, she thought it was a dress. The supple white fabric was so finely spun that it was nearly sheer. The hem and sleeves were meticulously embroidered with flecks of natural silver and something that resembled iridescent fish scales.

As she took it down from its place it floated like a cloud into her arms. It was, by far, the loveliest garment she had ever seen in her life. Using careful fingers, because it felt like any undue pressure might cause the gown to fall to pieces, she cast it gently onto the bed where it billowed in waves before settling onto the mattress.

With a considerable amount of regret, Jasmine glanced at the basin on the pedestal that her host had prepared earlier. Much to her surprise, the water still steamed inside the large reservoir and she imagined a tongue in cheek prayer to the faery king of hot water sprites as she stripped off her well-worn travel outfit, tossing aside the decimated blouse but neatly folding the leather.

She shivered a little shyly in the open room because her undergarments had fallen victim to the road a long time ago. Though she knew she was alone, so many living, breathing things in her bedchamber made her consciously aware that she was completely naked.

She lowered her head into the warm water first, and the moment it touched her scalp the muscles in her neck and shoulders relaxed.

Next to the basin was a stack of fresh, unbleached linen cloths and while it seemed a little strange to use them as a towel, they adequately wrapped around her dripping hair. After Jasmine had washed as best she could and folded the unusual pieces of linen around her body in the manner of a sarong, she approached the bed.

The white gown lay spread out like the figure of an angel should have been inside. Hoping that it would fit over her pitchfork and tail, she crossed her fingers and dropped the towels. After a moment of searching through the layers, she slipped the edge of the dress over her head.

It fell in gossamer waves over her shapely form, and though she was covered by fabric for the most part, Jasmine had never felt so undressed in her life. If only Hayden could see her in this gown. If she just had one more chance to be near him, she wouldn't let go for anything in the world.

All the worlds, I guess, she thought quietly as she tried to remember the way he had so tenderly held her hand against his cheek.

It was then she noticed the first real hitch in the costume. There were no shoes and somehow she didn't think her leather boots would match the ensemble. Fortunately, the floor of her room was soft and comfortable as she crossed to the vanity.

With an exaggeratedly graceful motion, she sat on the small bench in front of the dressing table. Strange and distant memories tugged at the corners of her mind and for a moment she felt like a small child, playing at her mother's things.

Her hands searched through the varied collection of cosmetics until they settled on a dark, onyx handled brush.

With slow and gentle strokes she began to work her way through the mass of damp, unruly hair, all the while humming a little tune. The melody was a simple one, and one she always comforted herself with as a child. When the brush had nearly completed its work, she gazed in the mirror with satisfaction.

It was at that very moment that the pale and drawn figure appeared alongside her reflection in the glass.

Jasmine spun around on her seat with panic, fully expecting the ghostly form to disappear when confronted face to face. Much to her dismay, the fragile looking woman remained in the center of the room.

The spirit seemed to be well dressed for a ghost, no doubt about that, but her gaunt appearance unnerved Jasmine and she sprang to her feet in defense.

She expected the visitor to cringe or back away at her reaction, but instead the light of her haunted green eyes began to shine with tears.

"My beautiful daughter," the apparition whispered, as she held a delicate hand out across the distance.

Chapter Thirteen

"Mother?" she spoke hesitantly, but after a minute she knew. The woman standing before her was every bit as lovely as the paintings that Lucas had done. In fact, she would have a hard time discerning the difference between their portraits. The moment she realized who this visitor was, the name Miriam entered her thoughts and she wondered how she could have ever forgotten it.

"You're my beautiful Jasmine," the thin woman said with tears in her eyes as she took a tentative step forward. "I was pleased that you chose to keep the name your father and I gave you upon your birth."

Jasmine wanted to tell her it was a coincidence, that the only reason she remembered that word was because of the flower she held so tightly in her hand the day her young world ended, but her argument fell flat before it left her lips. On the other side of the fountain, there weren't many coincidences.

"How did you come to be here?" she asked instead. She wanted to touch her, to ask her a thousand more questions at once, but she was afraid the fragile vision before her would fade away if she came on too strong.

"I am very ill, as Jacob must have told you," the beautiful woman explained with a longing look in her eyes. "Though I waited in that wonderful city by the river as long as I could. I came back to the God of the Grove for help and eventually accepted his offer to dwell here, for there is no passing time and I cannot grow any weaker."

"Why would he offer such a thing? Why does he care about dances and mortals or anything human at all?" Jasmine asked incredulously.

"Ever still my questioning and precocious child," she answered her with true pleasure, slowly extending her hand further to touch Jasmine's cheek. "Think on this ... If you were immortal and time meant nothing to you or your existence, would you not also crave the rituals and variance that we flawed creatures could bring?"

Suddenly Jasmine understood. The God of the Grove was honest when he told her he was not her enemy. In fact, he was nothing more than an immortal with an eternity stretched out before him and nothing else to do.

"If you're here, in his realm—" Jasmine took a moment to reason through her thoughts. "Where is my father?"

As soon as the words came out of her mouth, her mother's face fell and she lowered her head with sadness for one brief moment.

"My darling, your father was killed in the very first attack on the High King's compound. It happened during the first call to arms our kingdom had issued in three generations."

Thrown off balance by the answer, she abruptly sat on the edge of the bed in shocked disbelief. The worst part about all of this was that her father had never been in her dream, so she had no way to remember him or what he looked like.

"I feel his loss as deeply as anyone," her mother said in soothing tones. "He was everything in the world to me, but he didn't die in vain. Your father helped me secure the books of prophecy our people need to fight the Brotherhood of the Bane."

Jasmine's mind froze with an overwhelming thought and if she had gotten hit with a baseball bat at that moment she couldn't have felt more blind-sided.

"What was my father's name?" She barely spoke the words out loud, almost afraid to ask the question.

"Well, he was called Lucas." She smiled with a perfect memory of happiness on her lips and her waxy pallor colored with a soft blush. "His last words to me were that you two would meet again someday, but you wouldn't remember who he was."

Jasmine instantly wanted to cry with the news and her mind turned over all the possibilities of everything she might have done differently. To her own surprise, the ghost of a smile spread across her face instead of tears. Just a moment before, she thought she lost a father she had never known. Now she realized that she had plenty of memories of the man who found his true destiny with her mother.

Everything is falling into place, she thought to herself. Everything except her relationship with Hayden.

From somewhere in the distance, the perfect tone of a deep and resonant gong resounded and the echo lasted for what had to be miles. Jasmine was enthralled by the sound, the rich and vibrant note that shimmered through her body.

The lively fireflies that had nestled inside the vines overhead began to blink off and on in a brilliant light show as Jasmine followed her mother to the door.

"Are you coming to the celebration?" she asked the wisp of a woman next to her, hoping that she could spend a little more time with the mother she barely knew.

"This night takes place in the mortal realm. I cannot go, or time will pass for me."

"Then I will stay with you," Jasmine declared impulsively and stopped when they entered the hall.

"I have all the time in the world to see you, now that you're here." The beautiful woman set a reassuring hand on Jasmine's arm. "And we may thank our host for giving it me. I'm afraid it would be a slight to his ego if you didn't come to the gathering after all the interest he took in retrieving you."

She was disappointed that their reunion was so short lived, but she had to admit there was something to that argument. The God of the Grove was an unpredictable creature to say the least, and her mother's continued existence depended on his good favor. If she were to displease him now, a lot more than her own wellbeing could be at stake.

"When will I see you next?" She felt the tears behind her eyes, but they were not there to mark sadness. Instead, Jasmine felt like she could take on the world she was so filled with happiness.

"I think when we meet again you will find yourself embarking on your true path to the future ... Well on your way to becoming a woman of destiny." Miriam smiled benevolently as she reached along the wall and took down a softly luminescent globe of light that had nestled between two nearby branches.

Jasmine looked herself over a little in confusion as she took the newly plucked orb her mother offered without hesitation.

"I kind of thought I was a woman already." She gave Miriam a puzzled glance. "I mean, I have all the disgusting responsibilities that come with being one, anyway."

"And so you are, yet your heart is filled with the great mystery that is love," the wise woman added. "For now, you must follow the passage and seek the one who holds those answers."

Jasmine seriously hoped she didn't have to perform some kind of ritual to become a woman of destiny, like sticking her hand inside a tree stump filled with poisonous frogs or something. It was hard to imagine in this place what she might have to do.

"Follow this corridor to its end, and you will see the path you need to take," her mother instructed, and with a kiss on Jasmine's cheek she turned the other way.

Jasmine watched her walk into the distance until she was completely gone from view.

The ball of light she initially held away from her body was slightly warm and she was encouraged to cradle it closer. The gentle illumination it radiated cast everything nearby in a soft and romantic glow as she went down the passage. The corridor itself was not unlike the walkway to the gardens at the monastery and she found herself longing for the way that Hayden's arms had pulled her close and held her near his side.

She came out from under the natural canopy to find the moon was once again full and high in the sky. Shivering inside her gossamer gown, the silver light bathed her with an unearthly sheen as the silver flecks along her hem sparkled.

The smallest of breezes caressed her bare shoulders and as the fine fabric of her scandalously thin garment brushed against her body, she realized there was little between her skin and the elements tonight.

Jasmine glanced behind, in the direction she came, and saw that she had actually emerged from a set of giant roots at the base of a tree that seemed so big you could have built a city inside of it.

"Okay, let's remember where we parked," she said out loud in the clearing. She was well aware that she had left her more hardy clothing items, as well as her precious travel bag, tucked between the night stand and the bed back at the Best Big Tree Inn.

Her feet were still bare, but the trail of soft grass that urged her on was perfectly soft. She lost a great deal of confidence, however, when she saw that the wide inviting path led into a gathering of trees in the distance.

Jasmine strolled a little closer, but hesitated at the opening to the woods. There was an encouraging lack of mist along the trail, but even with her glowing orb in hand the way looked dark and creepy.

Just as she was beginning to consider turning back, the exquisitely deep, rich echo of the gong rang out again and she somehow knew that if it happened a third time she'd be awfully late and deep in trouble.

As if on cue, the trees ahead lit up with flashing fireflies, similar to the ones she had enjoyed in her room earlier. They sparkled in waves and patterns that were entrancing and before she knew it she had moved down the path and through the branches. If she was ever going to find Hayden, she had to keep going forward.

After she traveled a few yards into wooded area she noticed a tiny stream just ahead, running next to the trail. Jasmine was relieved to see the lightning bugs kept pace as she followed the pristine path, because it somehow made her feel like she wasn't so alone.

Initially she had gone slowly, afraid of stepping on a sharp stone or twig along the smooth dirt walkway, but she soon learned that there was nothing lying in wait to injure her exposed feet.

The stream widened more as she progressed further into the woods and Jasmine was pretty sure she knew what that meant, considering the nature of her host for the evening.

In just minutes her suspicions were confirmed. Ahead in the distance was a beautiful waterfall, but this display lay accessibly off the path. She curiously noted the water that spilled over the edge gave off a slight, delicate glow in an unusual shade of blue.

The fireflies went over near the cascade immediately, but she noticed that they stayed far enough to the side that they avoided the spray.

Following their lead, Jasmine stepped off the path despite everything she had learned in the past few weeks and made her way toward the falls.

Still a reasonable enough distance to be safe from the mist that clung visibly to the night air, she thought she could see a passage behind the cascade and was able to determine that the blue light source effecting the water came from within.

Jasmine decided she would be best off to scout a little further ahead before risking her neck on some slippery rocks, so she turned to go back the way she came.

She might have liked to be surprised that the trail now ended at the spot where she strayed, but the truth was that she almost expected that to happen. The only thing she wasn't sure of was whether she was making the path herself as she went along, or that it was guiding her in the direction she needed to go.

Either way, it looked like she was getting a shower.

"At least my non-existent shoes won't get wet," she grumbled to herself as she walked up to the face of the cave. The waterfall itself hung over the ledge a pretty fair distance so it turned out all she would have to do was take a nice little stroll underneath. That was all well and good, until she started in. The tiny droplets from the falling sheet of water clung to her curly strands of hair like a heavy veil.

Unfortunately for Jasmine, by the time she passed through and entered the interior of the cave, her hair was soaked and it clung to her face like the very image of a Grecian goddess.

Something a bit more disturbing though, she realized, was the fact that her thin gown now clung to every curve of her body like a glove.

She desperately tried to tell if the flimsy dress itself could be seen through in that condition, but the only light she had to go by was the strange glow from the crystals that formed at the opening of the cave, along with her personal orb that seemed to have faded considerably since it was plucked from its resting place in the hall. She pulled the slick fabric away from her skin as best she could and began to fan it back in forth in a useless attempt to dry the garment before she proceeded.

That was when the gong rang for the third time.

It was louder now, and the intense vibration from the echo along the cavern wall sent an involuntary shiver up her spine and her knees felt weak for just a moment. The resonance of the tone lingered deep within her bones for a minute before it dissipated and she knew she had better get a move on.

As she progressed further down the passage, the occurrence of natural crystal formations increased and more light was beginning to become available to her.

Initially she thought the stones themselves were the strange light source. However, she noticed as she went deeper within, that there was a patch of luminous moss at the base of each cluster and that was actually what gave off the feeble glow.

The quartz itself was veined through with shades of blue and purple and the color was absorbed by the fabric of her gown as it took on whichever hue she passed at the moment.

Whatever the dress was made of, she was relieved to discover it had nearly dried by the time she could detect the sound of voices ahead. She captured the wild curls that cascaded over her shoulder with her hands and inspected them in the cavern light. They faintly shimmered in her grasp like they retained a dusting of minerals from the falls, but appeared to fall in soft, natural waves down the bare skin of arms.

She thought about the hologram that she experienced before dinner at the monastery and wondered if this was something similar. She then recalled the time when Malcolm told her the God of the Grove used magic, not science, to perform his miracles. She had gotten drenched at the falls for real, and not at all when she was "Under the Sea."

She wasn't totally sure why, but for some reason the idea of magic was a much more romantic thought.

The sounds of laughter and exotic music echoed much more clearly through the tunnel, and she could see that there was an opening just ahead. Slipping through, she hoped no one would notice her late entrance.

Jasmine need not have worried; as she appeared inside the huge dome of the crystal cavern, she realized she was just one of many at the gathering and everyone swirled in dance to the music that filled the spacious area.

She looked to the ceiling in wonder because it was coated with a natural array of crystal chandeliers, though they were merely shards of colored quartz hanging in a delicate formations that dripped toward the floor with an elegant grace.

The luminescent moss grew all along the stone roof above, and Jasmine was aware in the back of her mind that she might never see such a spectacular display again.

The people who gathered to celebrate were lovely beyond compare. She looked at their magnificent costumes and realized that these simple folk must have spent the entire year making their garments for this celebration.

That was when she noticed everyone was wearing some type of mask—everyone except for her. She reached her hand up to touch the soft skin of her face and she realized she felt naked among the revelers who were so ingeniously disguised for the celebration.

Heads turned as those closest regarded her lovely face, and they gave her curious looks though she didn't feel any resentment from them.

She scanned the room for anyone who might seem familiar and was forced to see that many of the dancers had stopped to stare the longer she stood at the entrance to the tunnel, but from that moment on it didn't matter to her what anyone thought as her gaze fell across the cavern to a raised platform on the other side. That area was clearly for the nobles of the royal realm and they were dressed like a coronation was about to take place. She considered it to be strange that they all showed such a stiff example while their people celebrated at their feet.

That was the last thought to enter her mind, however, and it was immediately forgotten the moment she laid eyes on Hayden Edward Amarynn at the center of the crystal-encrusted ledge.

Chapter Fourteen

The crowd gave way much more easily than Jasmine would have thought as she carelessly pushed her way through. It almost felt like no one else in the world existed for a moment, until she was forced to notice the absence of music and the general increase of whispers throughout the cavern.

A wide path cleared before her and everyone's attention was on their Lord Amarynn, though it was obvious from Hayden's posture and manner he hadn't seen her yet.

Jasmine didn't care what they might be thinking about her; no words could possibly take away the feeling that gave her heart wings as she came to stand before her handsome prince in his formal blue military jacket. Cordelia immediately drifted close to the edge when she spied the source of all the commotion and her eyes lit with a vicious fury that could have no equal in any realm of existence.

"What are you doing here?" she hissed through clenched teeth, and her face became an alarming mask of jealous rage when she saw the exquisite gown that Jasmine wore and her luminous beauty.

All the while she was approaching Hayden appeared deeply lost in thought and unaware of his surroundings, but as Cordelia spoke he looked over at her then. When his gaze fell on her face, she saw the haggard look of disbelief in his eyes. It almost seemed as if he thought she was a vision and he looked around at the rest of the people gathered to determine if he might be dreaming.

"Jasmine," he spoke her name like it was sacred to him, and he moved toward her in amazement.

Before he could reach her at the edge of the platform, the God of the Grove mysteriously appeared at his side. The awesome figure of the immortal was clothed in white fabric spun from the same weave as her own gown, lined with silver on the edges. He wore a cloak of feathers as pristinely white as the newly driven snow and Hayden was visibly startled by his presence.

"Misplace something recently?" he inquired of his royal guest in the most polite manner, but Hayden's face came alive with emotion at the sound of his voice.

With a simple gesture, the God of the Grove motioned toward Jasmine, all the while keeping Hayden's ear.

"Will the royal bloodline completely falter now? Will you walk away from your kingdom for one woman?"

Prince Amarynn stopped short, and a shadow fell across his face as he turned to the intimidating figure in white.

"Your people already lose confidence in you, in your quest," he counseled in a reasonable tone. "Look at them all now. Look how they watch you to see which path you will choose. They saw you set aside your destiny to search for a girl, and your failure to recover the prophecies will be complete in their eyes if you choose poorly."

Jasmine couldn't believe what she was hearing. Her heart felt like it was tearing to pieces with each word her traitorous host spoke. She looked in Hayden's deep blue eyes, at the conflict he must have faced in her absence. Though it was just a few days for her in New Orleans, she had no way of knowing how long it had been for him.

She realized then it didn't matter what her heart wanted; she could never force Hayden to choose between her and his people. It was obvious to her now—that had been what he tried to protect her from all along, but in her usual headstrong manner, she fell in love with him despite his precautions.

Her eyes shone with the slightest hint of tears and the God of the Grove watched her curiously. He regarded both of them with intense interest, but no matter how much Jasmine tried she couldn't miss the sneer of triumph on Cordelia's face. If she called her out now, if she told the court and everyone at the gathering what Cordelia had done, it would look petty and weak in the face of her circumstances.

There was only one thing left to do, and so she did it.

Jasmine turned from the sparkling ledge, away from the God of the Grove and even Hayden himself. She thought if she ran quickly enough, she could get away from the gathering and everyone in it before they saw the tears in her eyes. If nothing else happened, Hayden would never know that she cried when she gave him up.

The same tunnel that she traveled through to arrive at this horrendous mistake of a celebration felt a lot longer during her retreat. Just like a terrible dream, it seemed to go on forever, but she kept at it. When she thought she would lose her breath entirely, she heard the waterfall up ahead.

If she could just rest a minute, she would return to the tree and seek out her mother. There was one person, at least, whose life she couldn't mess up any more at the moment.

The cave wall was damp this close to the spray, but she hardly cared as she leaned against the slippery surface. When she had stood on the forest path earlier the cascading water had taken on a blue tint from the cave crystals. Now, inside the tunnel, the evening moonlight made it appear as smooth as mercury as the tiny invasive water droplets found their way onto her skin once more.

Jasmine drew a few steady breaths and did her best to calm her trembling hands. She could see the fireflies through the watery curtain, waiting to follow her back to the tree. She pulled away from the supporting wall just as a breeze stirred behind her and she felt the chill of the water on her clothing then.

She was about to move closer to the cascade when a strong hand clasped her bare upper arm. Stifling a scream, Jasmine spun to face the intruder, ready for a fight.

Hayden immediately released her and she could tell by the look on his face that he was devastated that he had alarmed her.

"You can't follow me," she said, looking behind him into the darkness. She expected a multitude of villagers to come pouring through the passage in his wake at any moment.

"I can't?" He looked around, waiting for some reason. When no unwelcome spectators appeared her shoulders relaxed and she took in a deep breath of relief.

"I have something to say, but I don't know who is listening anymore," Jasmine started to explain. She wanted more than anything in the world to tell him about the books that Lucas had spirited away to New Orleans, but she couldn't be sure Cordelia or her sneaky brother might hear.

"You don't understand." His voice was strong and sure as he captured her hands in his and pulled her toward the falls like they might escape together. "I can't abide by any more rules. Without love, there is no future in my eyes."

His words cut deep into her heart and made it all the more painful for her. She jerked away from his grasp and darted beneath the water to the moonlight on the other side.

The pale rays glistened off her wet skin and she looked desperately for the path she knew was there just a short amount of time ago. There was no clear means of escape in view.

With no other choice, she slowly turned to face the mouth of the cave and the man who had followed her through.

Hayden stood with his back to the waterfall and his dark blonde hair was plastered to his cheeks. His dress jacket had definitely seen the worse for wear, and she watched with fascination as he unbuttoned it and cast it to the ground without a care. He wore a plain white tunic underneath the military garb and it clung damply to his impressive physique in short order.

Despite her resolution to be gone from his life and save him any conflict, she stood helplessly entranced as he approached her in the deserted glade.

"Please hear me." His voice was heavy with emotion as he took her hand and brought it to his lips with a reverent gesture. His eyes never left hers, and she could see that they burned with passion. "I have spent my entire life building a new world around my kingdom, for my people ... for my family." He paused then, and brought the back of her hand to his cheek just as she remembered. With a lingering sigh, he held her skin against him. "When I lost you, I knew that any foundation I built would be an empty one. It could never have meaning without you in my world."

"I don't want to come between you and your people," Jasmine whispered, but no one had ever said anything like that to her before in her life. It felt as if her heart was pierced when he spoke, his words were so sincere and true.

He stood back from her then, as if he might be changing stances, but she caught his sweeping gaze as it fell on her scantily clad form. His smoky blue eyes held her and she realized how revealing her costume must be after another trip through the spray.

"You're so beautiful I can't breathe," he said with barely

restrained intensity.

If Jasmine could give him her own breath she would have. If should could have ripped her soul out and handed it to him on a platter it would have been done immediately, but he already possessed it.

Her will to protect him was strong, but the heat that poured off his body was a temptation that drew her tentatively near no matter her resolve.

As if sensing her emotions, he reached out a slow hand and gently stroked the naked skin on her right shoulder. She shivered involuntarily and her back arched slightly when his hand made contact, her lips parting as the sensation ran through her veins to the rest of her body.

"Hayden." She whispered his name, fully intending to reason with him. It didn't matter what she was going to say; he swiftly pulled the words from her mouth with a deep kiss and she found herself responding with a fire that she never knew could exist inside her soul.

She slid the top of her thigh between his legs and pressed as closely as she could to his toned body.

His mouth released her lips for a moment and he moaned when she came up hard against him.

"Please," she said simply, aching from the separation of their kiss as she took his hands and slipped them inside the delicate fabric of her dress so that he touched her bare back.

Needing no further guidance, Hayden immediately ran his right hand up her spine and captured her neck in his strong grasp. Holding her there as he looked into her eyes, he slowly slid his other hand down low on her back and pressed her against his evident desire.

Jasmine gasped when she felt the pressure against her body, and the instant that breath left her mouth Hayden covered her swollen lips. The fragile fabric of her gown began to fall away as she strained against him, but she didn't care about that.

Hayden, however, did care.

"Not like this, not here in the open." He pulled his face away from hers and whispered in her ear. "Come away with me, come back to the monastery."

"It's always something," Jasmine groaned, but she learned a long time ago not to argue with him when he was doing what he thought was right for her.

"I will go anywhere you ask me to," she agreed with a sigh as she pressed her face against his neck. She could feel his pulse on her flushed cheeks and just knowing that his heart beat so wildly for her filled her with a renewed sense of desire.

Hayden pulled away from her with obvious regret, though he gave her a rather sultry smile as he adjusted the gown to cover her once again.

"We have to go get my things," she remembered, her head clearing a little once she was a few steps out of his embrace. "Follow me."

As she took him by the hand, the fireflies began to twinkle off and on again and as she caught them out of the corner of her eye, she noticed the path that she somehow missed before. They didn't get more than a few feet when she stopped and turned to him in excitement.

"Malcolm is here somewhere," she said to him suddenly, proud of the news when his face registered surprise.

"My Captain of the Guard?" he asked with disbelief, but she could see that he was delighted by the news.

"Don't you see?" She smiled when she remembered the favor she had asked of him in Ravenswood; it had actually benefited the captain as well, and she explained to him what happened at the cabin that second time around. "He did prepare his confession and begin the rift, but only because you spoke to him that day in the woods. He never got caught up in it."

"Because you saved him, probably his daughter, too," he finished her thought, looking at her like he never had any doubt that she was a super hero.

"Not if we don't get him out of here," she urged, and tried to remember which door he had been placed behind when they came to the end of the path and reached the big tree.

"My darling." He laughed as they entered the corridor. "If Malcolm is still in the realm of our immortal host, it is because he wishes to be. Don't think he hasn't escaped from here many times before."

"Come to think of it, he did say something along the lines that it would a cold day in the Grove if a certain 'someone' ever helped him leave a dimension …"

"I don't know how much of it he mentioned to you …" Hayden asked a little hesitantly, and she thought he might be bringing up a sensitive subject as she approached the door wreathed in Jasmine flowers. She slipped inside, feeling a little like a teenager after curfew.

"You can tell me of it, then," she teased him a little with a smile as they stood alone in the center of the room. It was pretty clear he didn't intend to deny her any wish, so he began the tale.

"Malcolm learned early on how to navigate this realm after one brilliant Candlemas celebration where he met his beautiful wife." Hayden had a smile on his face, remembering a time in his past.

"He courted Corrine in secret, over the course of many years. Finally, he convinced her to run away with him. Much to the surprise of everyone throughout the realms, the God of The Grove allowed her to leave."

"Why would he have to allow her?" Jasmine asked, and that feeling of sadness settled over her again when she thought about the fate of the mysterious woman.

"Because she was his daughter."

The words settled on her heart with a kind of sorrow and Jasmine sat on the edge of the bed for a moment, suddenly out of steam. "No wonder Malcolm was so devastated. After everything they had been through to be together, and he lost her."

Hayden sat next to her and put a strong arm around her shoulders.

"I know I took an oath to restore the prophecies of my people and I will do that, but I will do it with you at my side." He gently set his lips on her forehead. "I swear to you, as long as I have breath in my body, that we will always be together."

"In that case, I have something for you, Hayden Amarynn," she whispered in his ear. "Let me tell you a story of my own. It's about my father and a book shop in a city far, far away …"

•

"Do you mean to say that the entire time I was laying in that courtyard before you found me, those books were in the very next room?" The look he wore was uncertain, and for a moment she was afraid that he was unhappy with the news.

He stood and paced in front of the bed as a myriad of expressions passed across his face. Finally, a look of resolve settled there and he turned to her.

"I spent my life searching for these very tomes. After I met you, they were no longer the most important thing in my world and I set aside my quest to find the woman I love. And here you have brought them to me ..."

He came close to where she was sitting as his words dwindled away. Jasmine's heart began to speed up and he stood so near that she could catch the scent of his skin.

"Here you have brought them to me," he repeated the words in a husky voice. "And all I can think about is how damn beautiful you are sitting on the edge of that bed in your silken gown."

Suddenly his whole demeanor changed. Before, he was a man committed to his kingdom and pledged to his people. That responsibility had been lifted, and he appeared as nothing more now than a man who was free to give his heart.

"Do you still have the ring that I gave you?" he asked a little shyly, and she realized that he was nervous.

With a nod, she stood and pulled her bag from the crevice between the bed and the night stand. The silver circlet was just where she left it and with her back still turned to him, she pulled it from the little pocket.

As she held it in her hands, Hayden came up behind her and wrapped his arms around her shoulders.

Jasmine felt his sleek and muscular chest pressed up against her back and noticed that his shirt was a little damp still as it came in contact with her hot skin.

"Have you put it on yet?" he whispered in her ear, and not trusting her voice to respond she shook her head gently.

Hayden took the ring and cradled her fingers in the palm of his hands. With a subtle movement, he slipped it on her finger and she was surprised to find that it fit her perfectly. She leaned against him, her knees a little shaky after his actions.

He wrapped a supporting arm around her waist and set his right hand on her chest between her breasts. Her heart pounded like thunder the moment he touched her there, and her right hand flew up to press it tightly against her skin.

She leaned her head down and softly kissed his fingertips, rough and calloused from years of swordplay and fighting. His hand came alive on its own then, and he traced the outline of her swollen lips as gently as he could.

She took his other hand and slid it down the top of her thigh. She could feel his own heart throbbing hard against her back then, but he allowed her to run his fingers between her legs.

Despite her apparent confidence, Jasmine was trembling. She was so afraid of disappointing her prince that her hands betrayed her.

"You're my love, Lady Jasmine." His breath was torn and thick with passion. "And you will be my wife."

She wanted to turn and face him, to give him back some of the pleasure that was coursing through her body at his touch, but he held her strong and fast and she thought the ecstasy was more than she could take.

The knock was very secretive at first, almost surreptitious, and she thought if they just ignored it, it might go away.

It came again, and she was forced to acknowledge its presence when Hayden sighed heavily, gently releasing her.

She spun around in time to see him motion for her to be silent. He walked across the floor without making a sound, and braced his legs as he opened the door.

"If we're getting out, now is the time," the voice from the outer passage spoke with more than a little amusement.

Jasmine couldn't see the newcomer from her vantage point, but she had ears and it was clearly Malcolm in the hall.

"My friend," Hayden exclaimed warmly and led him inside. They clasped arms in greeting, and though Jasmine was a little breathless at the moment she was thrilled to see the look in Hayden's eyes as he stood before the Captain of the Guard once again.

"My Lady." Malcolm grinned cheekily in her direction, and she was compelled to look down and make sure her garments were in place. She didn't know if this dress would last the evening, but if it did, she planned to retire it somewhere to a place of honor among her things.

"I probably don't have to tell you that the place is in an uproar," Malcolm said, eyeing the couple with a smirk.

"If anyone would know, it would be you," Hayden replied smartly, and they both laughed.

"Get your things now, My Lady," the Captain spoke directly to her with an urgent tone. "You can change, or whatever you need to do, once we're in a safe place."

No one needed to tell her twice and she was out the door with the two men in less than a minute. She noted with regret that the fireflies that had trailed her during her stay were absent and it made her feel a little sad.

The trio broke away from the tree and hit the lawn at a steady pace when they discovered the forest ringed them tightly in.

"Damn, too late." Malcolm frowned and Hayden immediately stepped in front of Jasmine as a thick mist appeared at the base of the tree line.

"This definitely isn't a good sign," the Captain of the Guard added as the branches parted to reveal a path.

"Do we go down it?" Jasmine asked him, but he merely shrugged in answer.

"It depends on them ..."

She instinctively knew what he meant, but the hair on her arms raised just the same as she watched two figures stroll casually out of the gloom of the forest. Her heart skipped a beat when she recognized the God of the Grove, but it was his companion that gave her hope.

"Mother!" she exclaimed, and ran to the woman the moment they emerged.

"Mother?" Malcolm turned a questioning face to Hayden, but he indicated silently that he had no answers.

"It seems we're well blessed to have a wedding ceremony on this fine Candlemas eve," the God of the Grove spoke evenly, before turning his masked gaze to Malcolm.

"And this one will not be in secret."

The Captain of the Guard steeled his face against the last few words that were meant just for him. Despite his efforts, the emotion came through anyway and when it did, the immortal being nodded at him with acknowledgement.

"Prince Amarynn, did you swear a life oath to another while in the realm of the immortals?"

"I certainly did," he answered swiftly and surely, moving to stand at Jasmine's side.

"I assume you know the result of such a pledge made within the kingdom of the gods?"

"I certainly do." He grinned widely now and took Jasmine's hand as she stood next to her mother, only partially aware of what was going on.

"Then the two of you must wed before either may leave my realm."

"Oh, you're joking, right?" Jasmine finally took notice of the serious conversation, looking at each of their solemn faces in turn.

"He is not joking," Miriam assured her with a stalwart smile.

"I don't recall anyone asking me what I thought about all of this," she responded, her heart racing. No matter how many times she thought about Hayden and dreamed of him being in her life, she never dared admit to herself that she could belong to him in that way.

There was a moment of awkward silence and Hayden kneeled on the soft grass at Jasmine's feet.

"My Lady." He smiled, and she could see that he was the happiest he had ever been since they first met. "I have grown up and grown old thinking that my destiny lie among the lost books of my people, that I had to sacrifice my heart for a quest that would consume my very existence."

He raised her hand to his lips then, and though he lowered it after a kiss, he didn't relinquish his hold.

"I have grown up and I have grown old, but I see now that my destiny was meant to be shared with you. My true quest was to seek your love, and now I ask you to complete my soul. Will you grace my existence with the rest of your life?"

Jasmine didn't say anything at first. It wasn't because she was searching for an answer; it was because she couldn't think of any words to express it. After struggling with a few eloquent phrases, she finally settled on the one that fit her most.

"Let's do this thing."

There was a collective sigh of relief from the few people gathered and Hayden rewarded her with a smile that was worth more than any words she might have said.

"If I may, Jasmine," the God of the Grove addressed her informally, as always. "I'd like to bring one more guest to your wedding if you will permit it?"

"Who am I to argue?" she responded instantly, and as she did another figure came down the misty trail.

The young girl saw Jasmine first, and cried out with joy as she ran into the clearing.

"Jesi." She looked to Malcolm immediately.

He seemed frozen as the child stopped before him. She was every bit as beautiful as Jasmine remembered, even more so now in her Candlemas costume.

With a look behind her shoulder, Jesi made eye contact with her immortal grandfather. If Jasmine hadn't known any better, it seemed he actually gave her an encouraging look before she turned around and flung her arms around the Captain of the Guard.

"I know we haven't always seen eye to eye." Malcolm lifted a tear stained face to the God of the Grove. "But I thank you for this."

"Do not judge my regard for you so harshly," the masked figured said evenly in reply. "It is better to choose a mortal life filled with love, than to live with an eternity of its absence."

Those words let Jasmine understand why he let his daughter go. She also felt a deep sadness for the creature who had never known love.

"Shall we?" The solitary being moved onto the path. It opened wide and seemed a lot less ominous than it had a few minutes before. "The fountain waits."

Jasmine knew she should have been nervous as he led her to the place where the ceremony would be performed, but for the first time in her existence she felt like this was really her life. She felt like she was finally where she belonged.

The first thing she noticed when they entered the area was the agitated flickering of the fireflies she had come to miss. They seemed a little out of sync, but that wasn't the odd thing. Many of them emitted a slight shade of red, which was something she hadn't encountered in her time here. They nestled in the trees and appeared to be waiting.

The fountain at the center of the ceremonial glade was lovely beyond measure and she wandered close to the edge to see the floating candles and lilies when she stumbled over something heavy along the stone base.

She caught herself on the rim of the fountain before she fell over, but Jasmine quickly removed her hands in order to cover her mouth before she could cry out in alarm and startle anyone.

Lying at her feet was the contorted body of Lord Ference, clad all in black and curled up in a fetal position. She noticed with a kind of morbid fascination that his face and hands were covered with tiny little burns. His eyes were wide open and bulging, but the corneas were glazed over with a milky blue substance that told her he was quite dead.

Chapter Fifteen

The God of the Grove strolled over to the fallen lord whose own death mask was the very image of terror.

"You brought this on yourself, you know." He nudged him slightly with the toe of his boot before sighing. After a moment of consideration, he briskly snapped his fingers and walked away. Without a sound, several woodland ranger men melted from the outlying trees and into the garden.

They looked suspiciously like a gang of Robin Hoods to Jasmine, but the group seemed to know what to do as they lifted Ference's body and made off with it. She was glad they had him out of sight, but she wasn't sure if she would ever get that image of him out of her mind; the way his arms had been crossed over head, frozen in time, as if defending against something she couldn't imagine.

Jasmine looked around at the people gathered in the circle. They all seemed a little shocked by what they had seen a few moments ago, but none of them appeared to be grieving the loss of their fellow nobleman. Perhaps in a their own way they paid him a strange type of homage, their eyes lingering on the spot where he died, as they took a moment for a few private thoughts.

"The one thing that could have stopped you and no one knew about it," the God of the Grove said so softly that Jasmine wondered if she heard his words properly. Once her attention was drawn his way, he lifted his head and abruptly stepped before the couple.

"And now, I would like to present my gift to you both," he stated cryptically, and held up a hand the moment Jasmine began to protest that it was unnecessary. When her words fell silent, he pointed to the fountain.

Before their eyes, the makeup of the stone began to change. The ground at their feet morphed into flagstones and a sweetly scented vine wound its way among the guests that were present.

The scene was overwhelmingly familiar to Jasmine, and she clasped her right hand over her mouth to cover her reaction as they all witnessed a small girl lift her skirts in a delicate manner as she navigated the tangled courtyard to approach the edge of the fountain. As soon as Jasmine understood that she was seeing her dream, the figure of the young girl visibly stiffened.

"What is a lady doing out on the grounds, unescorted?" A young man's voice came from the outer edges of the vision and they all watched the beautiful young girl turn to meet this newcomer.

The handsome image of the blonde haired youth had lived in her dreams for so long that it had become a memory and she was not surprised at his reaction when he regarded the girl. But what she did see for the first time was the look of adoration and wonder in her own young eyes. Jasmine knew then that she had always loved him and there had never been any other option for her.

From the sidelines, Hayden still held her left hand tightly and he brought it to his lips though his eyes never left the scene being played out before them.

"This is a very special fountain," the young man continued as the vision progressed. "One that I am told will hold my destiny."

"What is your destiny?" the girl asked him in the very same way Jasmine remembered, her green eyes wide.

"A destiny must be discovered, my beautiful young girl." He gave her a brave smile, one that would tie her heart up forever and keep it until they could be together again.

The light in the courtyard slowly faded, and Jasmine found herself clutched tightly in Hayden's arms as the ceremonial glade took shape once more and the illusion ended with those last youthful words.

"I knew it was you," he whispered. "From the first moment I saw you again, on the night you saved me. I knew because you had my heart."

"Let the four directions be honored, as we call together the destiny of two souls," the God of the Grove said with a certain cadence, and Jasmine realized that he would perform the ritual that joined them together. Somehow it seemed fitting that he should do such a thing, and she hoped that it somehow eased his own heart.

Though he hadn't said it outright, she thought he had missed his own daughter's celebration with Malcolm.

"With the blessing of the hawk of dawn soaring through the clear blue sky, we turn to the East and call upon the spirit of air. With the blessing of the great stag in the heat of the chase, we turn to the South and call upon the spirit of fire. With the blessing of the dolphin of wisdom that dwells within the sacred waters of the pool, we turn to the West and call upon the spirits of water. With the blessing of the great bear whose strength flows from the fruit of the forests, we turn to the North and call upon the spirits of earth. May the harmony of our circle be complete."

Jasmine felt like she should be nervous, that she should wonder what her role was in all of this, but her heart was full of love and she felt like she completed a lifelong quest as much Hayden surely did.

"Who walks the path of the Moon to stand before all present and declare her love?"

The God of the Grove paused for an answer, but it wasn't until Jesi came up behind her and tugged on her sleeve that Jasmine understood she was on.

"I do." She said the first words that popped into her head. Luckily, they seemed to be the right ones.

"Who walks the path of the Sun to stand before all present and declare his love?"

"I do," Hayden responded instantly, and Jasmine was overwhelmed by the emotion in his voice as he turned to look in her eyes.

"As the grass of the fields and the trees of the forest bend together under the pressure of the storm, so you two must bend when the wind of change blows strong. May you both stand strong in each other's strength and may the warmth and light of your union be blessed."

Hayden grabbed her the moment the cheers began, and as he held her in his arms he gave her a kiss that made all his other attentions pale next to the intensity. He carried her to the edge of the fountain and slipped the ring off her finger while she was otherwise occupied.

"Hey," she protested, pulling her lips away, though she really didn't want to. "You gave that to me. You can't take it back."

"We're getting out of here," he whispered in her ear, and in a casual manner he flipped the silver circlet into the fountain.

It began to expand immediately and Jasmine looked in a panic at her guests in the clearing. Her mother seemed slightly shocked by Hayden's bold action, but Malcolm grinned in a knowing manner.

"Thank you," she said as quickly as she could to everyone present as the ring expanded rapidly.

On impulse, she disengaged herself from Hayden and came up to the God of the Grove.

"There are many times when I might have misjudged you, and I'm sorry for that," she said softly, and threw her arms around him with a haphazard hug.

Miriam gasped in spite of her manners, but quickly recovered as the immortal creature gently disengaged Jasmine's arms.

"And there are many time when you may not have." His eyes twinkled, and though she couldn't tell if he was serious, she finally knew he might have a sense of humor.

Unable to stand it any longer, Hayden captured her fingers and pulled her back to him as he covered her mouth with a kiss that made the world around them disappear. She entwined her arms around his neck and allowed him to sit her on the edge of the fountain.

Jasmine barely noticed the ring was active.

Chapter Sixteen

The slightest tingle swept through her body, but she was unable to tell if it was a result of Hayden's passionate touch or an effect of the ring. Silence filled her ears after a moment and she opened her eyes.

"Hayden." She pulled away when she realized she was still seated on the rim of the fountain in the glade. He put his fingers under her chin in an effort to catch her lips again, but she laughed as she evaded him.

"It didn't work." She playfully slapped him on the cheek. "Look, we're still in the clearing, only everyone has gone."

He stood then, and glanced around the empty area as she fished the tiny ring from the bottom of the fountain.

"I think you have to take this thing to the shop," she declared, turning the silver circle over in her hands. "Maybe I broke it."

"I don't care." He gave her a smoldering look. "As long as you're my wife and we're alone."

The fireflies nestled in the trees all around them, and their soft glow made Jasmine feel like a universe of stars had wrapped a blanket around the couple and given them the world.

She stood then, and entered his embrace willingly. This moment had been a long time coming and she knew that it was only the beginning.

Her back was to the empty path as he held her in his arms, so she didn't see what happened next, but as the rustling leaves and snapping twigs grew louder a sinking feeling grew in the pit of her stomach and she knew they had made a horrible mistake.

The ring had worked.

It had taken them back to the glade, some unknown time before the ceremony.

Jasmine broke free of Hayden's grasp in time to see Lord Ference as he rushed into the clearing with a shining silver dagger clutched tightly in his hand.

She tried to step in front of Hayden to protect him, but that was a foolish move because she was the one Ference wanted. He had her in his cold and deplorable grasp before she could blink, and that shiny dagger she saw a moment ago was at her throat.

"Wait, Ference," Hayden spoke in a voice that was so calm and reasonable that Jasmine was a little glad that he was the one doing the talking and not her.

"Lord Ference," her adversary sneered, pushing the blade closer to her skin. She could feel the sharp edge on her neck, but she kept her breathing as normal as possible so that it wouldn't cut any deeper than it had already.

"Did you think I would let you do this?" Ference growled, and his breath was stale on her cheek. She didn't dare to pull away, even though it repulsed her immensely.

"You soil the Amarynn bloodline with a commoner and pass my sister over whose lineage is more pure than yours!" He turned his face then and spat on the ground. "My grandfather would have led our kingdom to glory, but your family put him to the side—and all of it for this!"

The hand that held the dagger remained true, but the slippery arm around her waist reached up and grabbed a handful of her hair. She cried out despite herself, and the moment she did so the fireflies in the clearing began to emit an angry red glow.

A distinct hum began to vibrate throughout the glade, one that she had never heard before, and a fury of red lights flashed on and off from the trees.

Ference was half out of his mind, Jasmine thought, because he didn't notice the change that was happening all around them.

"Don't think I haven't instructed Cordelia." He laughed then, his whole body shaking. "You won't find her after tonight, but one day she will find you."

He raised his dagger hand high, as if he were building momentum. Hayden lunged forward then, knowing that if he didn't make a move at that moment it would be all over. He didn't reach Ference in time as the glinting dagger came down, but a thousand red fireflies did.

His scream was high and piercing, and the dagger fell from his nerveless fingers as the crimson glowing insects swarmed over his hand. The cruel fingers that wound themselves in her hair immediately released and clutched their burned counterpart. By then it didn't matter. A host of fire lit insects covered every exposed part of his body, every part except his eyes, so he could see the destiny he wrought upon himself as it happened.

Hayden grabbed Jasmine and wrapped his arms around her, though she could have told him they wouldn't be harmed if she had been able to catch her breath.

She watched with silent horror as Ference made his way to the fountain, possibly thinking of a way to diffuse the burn. He made it to the edge, but collapsed against the base of the stone. His arms crossed over his head and his eyes glazed over as he curled up against the bottom of the well.

She shivered with horrible recognition as he finally came to rest, holding the exact same position in which he had been discovered before the ceremony.

"They don't have lightning bugs like that where I come from," Jasmine said in a shaky voice, glad of Hayden's arms to support her until she could regain her equilibrium.

"Yes they do," he reminded her in a strong and sure voice. "This is your world, Jasmine. You're finally home."

She realized then, through everything that happened, the silver ring remained clutched in her fist. Slowly, her fingers uncurled and she looked at it with a little apprehension.

"If it's all the same to you, I think I'd rather walk to our honeymoon." She indicated the clear path leading away from the glade.

"I will go anywhere you ask me to." He repeated the same passionate words she spoke to him earlier.

Jasmine could only be sure of one thing as they joined hands and set upon the path, not really knowing where it would lead: their destination would be exciting without a doubt, but now that they were together, they had destiny at their fingertips and the future would be the story of their love.

•••

Kimberly Adkins

Kimberly Adkins resides in Nashville, Tennessee, Music City USA. She is an avid artist who works with oils, acrylics and water colors. She also spends time song writing and sometimes singing—but only when forced! She has always loved Egyptian lore, as well as science fiction and fantasy. For Kimberly, writing romances is a wonderfully appealing outlet for "magic and passion."

www.KimberlyAdkins.com

Also by Kimberly Adkins ...

A Darkly Enchanted Artifact.
A Passion to Outlast the Centuries.

ISBN: 978-0-9793252-3-6
$12.95 paperback
$6.00 Ebook (PDF format)

Two more paranormal romances you might love!

Sofia never believed the words on the parchment to be more than myth. Until one winter morning changes everything. Now the breathtaking man who haunts her waking hours is the very soul whose immortal curse she must put an end to - one way or another.

ISBN: 978-0-9793252-2-9

Deep in a box of used books, counselor Tory Sasser comes across a novel without an ending: Heatherfield. She reads the story of scarred war veteran, Jake Benjamin, a fictional character in a fictional town. Or is he? Tory is desperate to find her way back home to reality. Yet what is more real than true love? No, Heatherfield isn't all it seems ... not at all.

ISBN: 978-0-9793252-8-1

www.ingramcontent.com/pod-product-compliance
Lightning Source LLC
La Vergne TN
LVHW090944080826
845145LV00003B/878